Reviewers and readers love
PAMELA BRITTON!

"NASCAR fan or not, let *In the Groove*
drive you to distraction."
—*Romantic Times BOOKreviews* (4 stars)

"A fairy tale that succeeds."
—*Publishers Weekly* on *Scandal*

"This is the kind of book that romance fans
will read and reread on gloomy days."
—*Publishers Weekly* on *Tempted*

"Passion and humor are a potent combination…
author Pamela Britton comes up
with the perfect blend."
—*Oakland Press*

"This nonstop read has it all–sizzling sexuality,
unforgettable characters, poignancy, a delightful
plot and a well-crafted backdrop."
—*Romantic Times BOOKreviews* (Top Pick)
on *Tempted*

"It isn't easy to write a tale that makes
the reader laugh and cry, but Britton succeeds,
thanks to her great characters."
—*Booklist* (starred review) on *Seduced*

Dear Reader,

It's hard to believe that my Rodeo Wranglers series is at an end. It seems like just yesterday I was planning each book. Now here we are, and the series is over. Where has all the time gone?

I hope I've saved the best for last. *The Cowgirl's CEO* is a definite change of pace from my other Rodeo Wrangler stories. Each of my previous books featured hunky cowboys, but this time I turned things around a bit and wrote about a cowgirl.

I hope you enjoy Carolyn and Ty's story, and that you've had fun spending time with the townspeople of Los Molina. It might interest you to know that Los Molina is based on my own small hometown of Cottonwood, California. I've even been so bold as to steal *real* business names such as The Elegant Bean, our local espresso shop, which is where I write my books. (If you're ever in town, stop by!)

If a trip to Northern California isn't in your plans, please stop by my Web site at www.pamelabritton.com. Or "friend" me on Myspace: www.myspace.com/pamela_britton.

Thanks for riding along with me. As one of my heroes might say, "It's been a real pleasure, ladies and gentlemen!"

Pamela Britton

The Cowgirl's CEO
PAMELA BRITTON

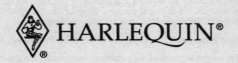

TORONTO • NEW YORK • LONDON
AMSTERDAM • PARIS • SYDNEY • HAMBURG
STOCKHOLM • ATHENS • TOKYO • MILAN • MADRID
PRAGUE • WARSAW • BUDAPEST • AUCKLAND

ISBN-13: 978-0-373-75170-9
ISBN-10:   0-373-75170-2

THE COWGIRL'S CEO

www.eHarlequin.com

Printed in U.S.A.

ABOUT THE AUTHOR

With over a million books in print, Pamela Britton likes to call herself the best-known author nobody's ever heard of. Of course, that's begun to change thanks to a certain licensing agreement with that little racing organization known as NASCAR. Nowadays it's not unusual to hear her books being discussed by the likes of Jay Leno, Keith Olbermann or Stephen Colbert. Flip open a magazine and you might read about her, too, in *Sports Illustrated, Entertainment Weekly* or Southwest Airlines' *Spirit Magazine.* Channel surf and you might see her on *The Today Show, Nightline* or *World News Tonight.*

But before the glitz and glamour of NASCAR, Pamela wrote books that were frequently voted the best of the best by the *Detroit Free Press,* Barnes & Noble (two years in a row) and *Romantic Times BOOKreviews* magazine. She's won numerous writing awards, including a National Reader's Choice, and has been nominated for Romance Writers of America's Golden Heart.

When not following the race circuit, Pamela writes full-time from her ranch in Northern California, where she lives with her husband, daughter and, at last count, twenty-one four-legged friends.

Books by Pamela Britton

HARLEQUIN AMERICAN ROMANCE

985—COWBOY LESSONS
1040—COWBOY TROUBLE
1122—COWBOY M.D.
1143—COWBOY VET

HQN BOOKS

DANGEROUS CURVES
IN THE GROOVE

This one's for my husband because it's been
a while since I've dedicated a book to him even
though, truth be told, they're *all* for him.
I know you're reading this, Pooh Bear,
because I always see you sneak a peek at this page
(and you thought I wasn't paying attention!).
Thank you for always being there to give me
the man's perspective, and for coming up
with silly plot devices that turn out to be not so
silly after all, and for all the other things
you do that are too numerous to list.

I <3 U!

Chapter One

The horse reared.

"Easy there," Caro said, her chest making contact with the paint's mane. She tightened her legs, holding on. "Whoa," she added, her black cowboy hat almost falling from her head.

Thumper came back to earth with a snort and a shake of his black mane, only to spin around. Caro did her best to point toward the narrow alley that led to the arena—and Thumper's freedom.

"Easy there, boy," she said, jamming down her hat.

The gelding half reared again, his mouth working the bit, flecks of foam landing on his sweaty chest. Fifteen hundred pounds of horseflesh tensed, muscles at the ready, all waiting for one thing: Caro to let him go.

"Not yet," she told him, glancing left.

He was still there.

She'd noticed the man during her warm-up. The indoor sports complex didn't have a big practice pen, and since only rodeo competitors were allowed behind the chutes, spectators were rare. He stood out like a tick on a hound in his brown sports coat and beige cotton slacks. His tan cowboy hat shielded his eyes from her view at the moment, but they'd been trained on her the whole time she and Thumper had been loping around the ring. Eyes as black as the hair beneath his hat.

The roar of the crowd caused Thumper to lift his head, ears pricked forward. The rider on course was nearing the end of her run. Caro couldn't see inside the arena; the sports venue had been built for basketball and hockey, not cowgirls and cowboys. She and Thumper were tucked around a corner, so that when it was their turn to run, they'd have to race through a narrow corridor lined with aluminum fences, veer left and *then* crank up the speed.

Thumper lunged. Caro checked him again. Linda charged out of the tunnel right then.

Time to go.

The gate man called her number over the roar of the crowd. "One seventy-nine!" Caro could hear the voice of the rodeo announcer, but was too far away to catch how good a run Linda had had.

"Easy, boy," Caro said, because she could see Thumper's shoulder twitch, a certain sign he was about to erupt.

All right, Daddy, Caro prayed. *Here I go again. Help me out if you can.*

She applied pressure, and that was all it took. A simple squeeze. No kick, no leather strap, nothing. And even though she expected it, Caro's upper body still jerked back, her hat almost knocked off again. The paper number pinned to her back rustled. She righted herself about the time she passed by the man who'd been watching her, her left hand on her hat, holding it in place. The arena opened up before her. She focused, not even hearing the screams of the fans. Thumper's stride grew long. There it was: the first barrel.

Three…two…one…

They began to turn, Thumper's hooves digging into the ground. The smell of dirt filled her nose as they leaned and tilted some more, lower still….

Her knee brushed the barrel.

She gasped. The obstacle rocked. She stretched out her arm and tried to right it, but couldn't reach it. And now Thumper was moving on to the second barrel. Had the first one fallen? She didn't know. Couldn't look back. Rodeo fans rose to their feet as she careered toward the next obstacle.

Three…two…

Too fast. She tried to pull up. Thumper didn't respond, but began his turn. It felt like being on the end of a yo-yo. Caro hung on the whole trip around, and when she looked up, she could see the first barrel. It still stood.

Thank God.

One more to go.

She thrust her upper body forward, her silky shirt with its glittering rhinestones glistening beneath the arena lights. This would be the longest run. They'd have the most speed, too, and so the timing needed to be perfect.

Three…two…one…

There. Perfect. She leaned once more. Thumper shifted, too. It felt fast.

Bam.

Her knee again. Damn it. She shot a glance back as they charged away.

The barrel stood!

Thank you, Lord, she breathed, closing her eyes for a split second. When she opened them again, she and Thumper were halfway down the arena. She could feel the saddle hit Thumper's back. Thump, thump, thump…her reason for naming him. Faster and faster. The wind made her eyes tear. And then she and the gelding dashed through the electronic beams that tracked the elapsing seconds.

"Thirteen point forty-three!" she heard the announcer say. "Wow! That's our best time right there, ladies and gentlemen. Caroline Sheppard is leading the barrel racing…."

She tuned the words out. *Fast time.* That was all she'd needed to hear. But would it hold up?

Thumper resisted when she pulled back, but Caro demanded he obey. He slowed. They passed beneath the concrete archway and into the tunnel, turned right. "Whoa," she ordered.

Reluctantly, Thumper did as asked. "Good boy," she said, patting his neck. He was dripping with sweat.

"Nice run," Melanie said from the back of a horse that was rearing and snorting as badly as Thumper had been.

"Thanks." Caro trotted past her toward the warm-up arena. She glanced around. Her male friend was gone.

Thumper finally decided to walk, so Caro loosened the reins. Her horse dropped his head, his sides expanding and contracting as he fought to catch his breath. She breathed heavily, too, the adrenaline of running barrels a high that never ceased.

And there he was.

She stiffened in the saddle. The man blocked her path. How had he got into the competitors' area?

"Caroline Sheppard?" he asked.

Green. His eyes were green, not black, after all. A soul-piercing, breath-stealing green. The guy looked up at her as if he owned her—and in a way he did. Tyler Harrison, she realized. Owner of Harrison's Boots. The Harrison name was synonymous with quality boots, recognized the world over. The name was also on every piece of equipment she owned: her saddle pad, her horse trailer, her truck. Harrison's was her sponsor, and she could tell by those eyes that Tyler Harrison was *seriously* displeased.

Maybe she should have returned his calls—all ten of them.

She was stunning.

Ty had known that. When his PR department had shown him pictures of her all those months ago, he'd realized immediately what a gold mine they'd have if she made it to the Wranglers National Finals Rodeo—the NFR. And here she was, just a few weeks away from doing that very thing.

But what the photographs hadn't told him was that in person her hair was as gold as summer wheat. And that her grayish-blue eyes glowed with passion. Sitting on her horse earlier, the black-and-white gelding doing his best to unseat her, she'd looked magnificent. Like something out of the Old West: fearless, proud, determined. Ty had been unable to keep from staring at her as she'd rode her pattern, flawlessly guiding her horse around all three barrels.

She excited him.

He hadn't expected that, wondered if it might be a problem. But, no, he quickly reassured himself. It wouldn't be. He was good at keeping his head on straight when it came to business matters, and he definitely had business with Ms. Sheppard.

"Mr. Harrison," she said, with a smile that could only be called impatient. "Why didn't you tell me you were coming to New York?"

She'd recognized him. Surprising. They'd never met, although he supposed his picture had appeared in enough western magazines that she might have seen his photo a time or two.

"You know why I didn't tell you I'd be here."

She looked guilty, then contrite and finally amused. "You going to arrest me then?" she asked. "Am I in trouble for failure to return a sponsor's calls?"

"Your horse looks as if he needs cooling down," he answered brusquely, unwilling to play along. He was still peeved. They'd spent thousands of dollars supporting her rodeo career this year. The least she could have done was call them back. But they'd been trying to track her down for weeks. Rodeo performers, he'd learned, were as fickle as the wind. They could enter two, three, sometimes five rodeos a weekend—but they didn't always show up at them. Figuring out which ones Caroline Sheppard had entered had been like throwing darts at a board.

"Let me slide off," she said, dropping her reins before swinging her right leg over the saddle and slipping to the ground.

She was tiny. When he'd seen her out in the arena, her lithe body clinging to her horse, blond hair streaming behind her like the tail of the horse she rode, she'd looked tall. But clearly that had been an illusion. Standing beside him, she barely came to Ty's shoulder.

"Look," she said, "I've been busy. Making it to the NFR is the most important thing in the world to me."

"More important than your sponsor?"

She winced, patting her horse's neck as they went through an opening in the pipe panels. "I don't really have time to go off and film a commercial or talk to reporters or whatever else you have planned for me."

"It's part of the contract," he said, resisting the urge to add that she was currently in breach of that contract.

"I know that," she said, pausing for a second along the rail. "But can't we do it later?"

"No, we need you to film the commercial now. Before you make it to the NFR."

"*If* I make it."

"You will."

"Not if I'm off filming a commercial."

She stumbled on a clod of dirt. He steadied her. Mistake.

"Thank you," she said.

He released her, clenching his hands afterward.

"The dirt they truck in for a rodeo is never any good," she said. "It clumps together like kitty litter."

"I see that," he murmured.

He'd *wanted* to meet her face to face he suddenly realized. Had been fascinated by her photo. After watching her ride, he found his interest had only grown.

"We'll do everything we can to make this easy on

you," he said. "We're not asking you to fly off and film the commercial at a different location. We'll come to you. We just need a few hours of your time."

She watched a horse and rider walk by. Ty followed suit, their gazes meeting again as she said, "Just a few hours." Her shoulder brushed her horse's neck.

She was beyond pretty, he thought. Gorgeous was a more apt word. And as he stared down at her, the idea popped into his head that perhaps his interest in her was bordering on personal.

"Will you commit to that?" he asked.

"Sounds like I don't have a choice."

They'd made it to the warm-up arena he'd been watching her in earlier. She stopped outside the gate.

"You're right. You don't," he said, out of patience. "The NFR is in less than a month. We need to get the commercial in the can well before then."

She didn't say anything, just continued to appear irritated.

"When do you have to leave for your next rodeo?" he asked, pulling out his Blackberry.

She let loose a long-suffering sigh. "I'll be in Louisiana on Saturday."

He checked his schedule. "Then I guess Louisiana it is."

She shook her head, fiddling with the reins. "Saturday morning. That would be the best time. Before the rodeo starts."

"Saturday," he said. "I'll see you there."

Chapter Two

I'll see you there.

Caro replayed the words during the long drive to Louisiana. She kept hoping the damn man would call to cancel. Instead, all she'd received was a message from his director informing her that they'd be on location by Friday so they could "get the commercial in the can" on Saturday.

Terrific.

The last thing she wanted, or needed, was a bunch of people getting in her way—not to mention one bossy, overbearing man—while trying to qualify for the NFR. Granted, Tyler Harrison had good reason to be upset with her. Once he'd walked away she'd realized she had no one but herself to blame for her current predicament—but that didn't mean she had to like it. Filming a commercial now would be a serious distraction, not to mention, inconvenient. Not only was she set to ride in Louisiana, but she was also competing the same weekend in Houston, at a non-PRCA rodeo, which meant once she finished riding in Lousiana, she'd have to pull up anchor and drive.

"Hey, Caro," Mike, one of the best team ropers she knew, called out after she'd pulled into the Louisiana sports complex. He grinned and waved, his big belly hanging over his belt buckle. "Heard you're gonna be a TV star."

Caro slid out of her truck, slamming the door with more force than necessary. She'd parked in the livestock area, out behind the arena. The afternoon sunshine refracted off the polished aluminum of her trailer, causing her to squint in discomfort. She wasn't scheduled to compete until tomorrow afternoon's slack, but there was still plenty to do today. She had to unload the horses, bed them in their stalls, feed and water them. Then she needed to ride, maybe even offer to ride horses for other people—an easy way to make an extra buck. Despite her big-name sponsor, she was still always short on cash.

"Yeah," she said, stopping alongside her trailer. She had all three barred windows open to let her horses peer out, their nostrils flaring as they took in the new surroundings. "And I can't wait," she muttered sarcastically.

Mike hugged her to his side. The big man had always treated her like a younger sister since their days riding the college circuit together. He all but tickled her ribs before letting her go.

"Aww," he said, tipping his tan hat back, breaking into a jowly smile. "You'll do great."

"Don't know about that." And to be honest, she *didn't* know; she was nervous about the whole thing. Funny, she hadn't realized it until that very moment.

She watched as Mike ducked into his trailer. One of the horses inside her rig nickered—probably Classy, her second-string barrel horse. A chain inside Mike's trailer rattled, then came the unmistakable sound of a horse backing out, the heavy clumping of hooves like multiple strikes of a rubber mallet. A big-shouldered chestnut appeared, rear end first, and then Mike himself.

"Who's this?" she asked.

"Terminator."

"Excuse me?"

Mike's blue eyes twinkled. "The guy that used to own him called him that because he's so big muscled—like Arnold Schwarzenegger."

Caro just shook her head.

"But back to your commercial," Mike said, sliding his hand down his horse's leg. No doubt he was checking for heat or swelling, since horses sometimes injured themselves in trailers. "You've done Harrison's Boots a favor by signing on as their spokesperson. With your looks, all you'll have to do is smile to sell their new line of western boots." He straightened, still holding the end of the lead rope. "But it sure looks like a major production over there. Heard a few of the guys complaining, but I guess when you're a big-name company like Harrison's, you can pull a few strings."

"Major production?" Caro asked.

"There's a bunch of television equipment out by the practice pen. Someone told me it was for your commercial."

"Really?"

Mike tipped his head toward the arena out beyond the portable stables. "Go on over there and check it out."

"I think I will," she said, patting the trailer. "Keep an eye on the guys for me, will you?"

"Sure thing," Mike said, squatting down to check his horse's other leg.

She had to walk through a sea of horse trailers, and then the portable stalls. The white canvas lining them appeared almost gray in the shadow of the big building. When she rounded the end of the aisle, she halted in her tracks. "Holy—!" she muttered.

On the other side of the arena, scaffolding held various lights and film equipment, among other equipment she didn't recognize. But it wasn't just that. No. There was *snow* on the ground, or what looked to be snow. It covered the blacktop—piles of it heaped up, with fake pine trees stuck in it. Every horse in the area was fussing and snorting. A few animals refused to walk forward when they caught sight of not just the snow, but the men and women working up on the scaffolding. To horses, those people probably look like giant, equine-eating monsters.

"What are you doing?" she asked the first person she came across, a tall man wearing a dark suit, his head tipped back as he looked up at the scaffolding.

"Ms. Sheppard," he said, turning, some undefined emotion flickering for a second in his green eyes. "When did you arrive?"

Tyler Harrison. She had to work hard to keep her surprise from showing. Today he appeared almost intimidating in his dark gray suit and tie.

"Mr. Harrison," she said. "I, uh, I just got here."

"You're early."

"Yeah. I was on the road by 5:00 a.m."

"Well, I'm glad you arrived safely. I just got here myself."

"You might not be so glad when you hear what I have to say."

"Are you unable to do the commercial?" he asked, the space between his eyebrows pushing together.

"No, no. It's not that. It's just that you're scaring every horse within a fifty-mile radius."

"Excuse me?"

She pointed with her thumb. "Look at them."

He peered through the myriad equipment. Several horses in the arena were snorting, a few of them sidestepping. Granted, a couple were loping around as if it was no big deal, but the less seasoned animals were definitely acting up.

"I see what you mean," he said. "To be honest, when I saw the location of the set, I wondered if that might be a problem."

"Mr. Harrison?" A small man in a red 49ers cap appeared. The acne on his face proclaimed him to be barely out of puberty. "We're ready to test the snow blower."

"The snow—" Caro shook her head. "You can't shoot fake snow into the air. That'll only make things worse. Someone'll get dumped the minute you turn that thing on," she added.

He glanced toward the arena, the wrinkles between his eyebrows deepening. "I've no doubt you're right, so we'll wait to test it until nobody's in the arena." Tyler turned to the snowblower guy. "Give me a second."

"Sure thing, Mr. Harrison."

"This arena will never be empty," Caro said, watching as the man walked off. When she glanced back at Harrison, she caught him staring at her chest. Instantly, her hackles rose. She hated when men ogled her breasts, which were embarrassingly large, given her small frame. She was just about to give him a piece of her mind when she realized he was reading her T-shirt, at least judging by the smirk on his face.

Cowboys Are Like the Circus: Too Many Clowns, Not Enough Rings.

He met her gaze again, one eyebrow arched.

"People ride their horses here at every time of the day," Caro added, blushing. Well, now he knew how she felt about cowboys. Actually, not just cowboys, but men in general. "There'll be competitors rolling in from every part of the country, at all hours. But it's not just the horses and riders. What about the livestock?" She pointed to the pipe pens not far away, where bulls and steers were calling out to each other. "You'll set them off, too."

"Then we'll film after the rodeo tomorrow. Surely the animals and competitors will be loaded up and gone by then."

The enormity of his ignorance astounded her. She had no idea why she'd thought he knew anything about the sport. Because he seemed so in charge of everything, she'd assumed he'd done his research. Apparently, that wasn't the case.

"This rodeo is three days long. It starts tonight and goes on through Sunday."

"But you said you perform tomorrow."

"I do. But there's also slack. That's a part of the rodeo fans don't get to watch. So you have that going on in the early afternoons and then performances in the evening. The livestock will be here though Sunday, maybe even Monday, depending on the stock contractors."

She saw Harrison's eyes narrow. He glanced around, his chiseled jaw more pronounced from the side. He was handsome, if you were into city slickers. She wasn't.

"I wasn't aware of that," he said.

"So I presume." *Terrific.* Just what she needed. Not only would she be distracted by his film crew, but she'd have to educate Mr. Harrison, too.

"There'll be people around here for hours. And if you turn on your snow machine, you'll have a riot on your hands."

"But we were told it was okay to film here."

"Rodeo performers—or rodeo personnel—won't care if you were given approval by the pope himself. And they'll care even less when you start using fake-snow machines."

"You're probably right."

Her shoulders stiffened when she saw Walt Provo, the rodeo's manager, walking toward them, the series logo on his white shirt.

"Caroline," he said, tipping his black hat.

"Walt."

"You in charge here?" he asked her companion.

"Ty Harrison," her sponsor said.

Ty? She wouldn't have expected him to shorten his name, not with the way he looked and dressed. Like a Wall Street playboy. All he was missing was a pair of dark sunglasses.

"Mr. *Harrison?*" Walt said. "You one of the Harrison family?"

"I am."

Walt didn't seem very impressed, just nodded and said, "I'm Walt Provo. PRCA."

Professional Rodeo Cowboys Association. Walt

had worked for the organization as long as Caro could remember. The man was so wizened and stooped he resembled a candy cane stuck in a sugar cube standing there on top of the fake snow.

"Biodegradable rice flakes," Ty said, following her gaze.

"Really?" she asked, surprised. It looked like fresh powder.

"Speaking of snow, we've had a few complaints," Walt said.

"Caroline was just telling me that," Ty said.

"Well, good. Then you know what the problem is." Walt lifted his hands. "Before you say it, we know you were given permission by the facilities manager to film—" Walt's radio squawked. He glanced down at the device on his belt and lowered the volume. "As I was saying. I know you were given permission to film here, but that's typical. It's the same story at every indoor sports venue. The city slickers who run the place don't know squat, and tell people to do things willy-nilly, without giving a thought to the animals. We have to intervene from time to time—like now."

"He has a snow machine," Caro said. "He wants to blow his rice flakes around."

"You have a *what?*" Walt asked, gray brows arching almost to the brim of his cowboy hat.

"Not over the whole set. Just right here, where Ms. Sheppard will be leading her horse for part of the commercial." Ty pointed out a strip of pavement left pretty much uncovered, with bare asphalt peeking through. "The flakes come out of a hose, which we were attaching to the scaffolding up there," he said, pointing above their heads. "It'll look like it's snowing when it's on."

Walt shook his head. "*Not* a good idea. Some of our animals might be used to television cameras, but I'll wager none of them have seen rice flakes blown by a machine."

"I see your point," Ty said. Caro thought his eyes really were a pretty green. And intense. When he looked at her, she felt like he was seeing her through a telescope.

"Can you relocate farther away?" Walt asked.

"Negative," he said, sounding every inch the executive. Definitely *not* her type.

"It took us half the morning to set up," he said. "To move it would delay things beyond an acceptable parameter." His gaze slid her way. "And we're on a tight schedule."

"Then I guess we'll have to close the practice pen," Walt said.

"But what about the people who still need to practice?" Caro asked. *Like me.*

"No worries," he said. "Tonight's slack doesn't start for a few hours yet. We'll move everyone inside for practice. You'll have an hour until slack starts, to finish setting up. But once we let people back into the arena, you'll need to stop moving things around."

Caroline relaxed, at least until he opened his mouth again.

"Can you film your commercial now? It'd make it easier on everybody if we could get this over with today. Everything could get back to normal before the bulk of the competitors arrive."

"Today?" Ty asked in obvious surprise, his expression no doubt mimicking her own. "That's not doable. Not only are none of the camera crew on hand, the director isn't due to arrive until later tonight."

"I see." Walt shook his head and sighed. "All right then, Mr. Harrison. We'll do what we can to accommodate you."

"Appreciate that, Mr. Provo."

"Just out of curiosity, when *were* you planning on filming?" Walt asked.

"Tomorrow morning," Ty said, at the same time as Caro.

"Early," she added.

"Then I'll be sure to alert management. I'll have someone close the practice pen in a moment or two, and then early in the morning as well."

"Sounds good," Ty said.

"'Preciate your cooperation, Mr. Harrison." He tipped his hat, talking into his radio the moment he turned away.

"Wait," Ty said. "If by some miracle I *do* manage to get everyone lined up, how do I get hold of you?"

Walt clipped his radio back at his waist. "Caro knows how to reach me. Just let me know."

"There's no way we can film today," Caro said after Walt had gone. "I have horses to unload and ride."

"I realize that," Ty said. "But it sounds like Walt would be happier if we did it today. And to be honest, Ms. Sheppard, my director had doubts that we'd be able to finish up in one day, anyway. If that happens, and we film on Saturday, we might be forced to do a second shoot at another rodeo, and I doubt you'd want that."

"No, but—"

"Let's try to get this done today."

"But I—"

"I'll let you know."

He turned away, striding over to the guy in the ball cap who, she suddenly realized, had been waiting there the whole time.

Damn it. She hated bossy, autocratic men.

It's only a couple of hours, Caro. It's not the end of the world.

But she had a feeling she'd be dealing with *this* bossy, autocratic man for *way* longer than a day.

Chapter Three

She didn't look happy.

Ty told himself he shouldn't care. Ultimately, Caroline Sheppard was responsible for their current predicament. If they were on a tight schedule it was her fault. And if they were forced to do the shoot today, she would just have to deal with it.

But he *did* care.

He hated playing the heavy. Especially with Caroline. And that perplexed him.

He glanced her way again. Guy—the key grip—was waiting for instructions about the snow machine. "We'll have to wait to test it," he said, his eyes following her progress back toward the barn, her loose, beautiful hair, which swayed back and forth with every step. "They want to clear the arena."

"Roger," Guy said. "We'll keep working on the lighting."

"No, don't," Ty told him, his eyes still on Caro. "Wait until they clear the arena."

"Will do."

Caroline rounded the end of the barn, out of sight. *Remarkable woman,* Ty found himself thinking. Gorgeous. A champion barrel racer. College valedictorian.

If they'd met under different circumstances, he might have considered pursuing her.

He reached for his cell phone. "Get me Bill Clement," he ordered his executive assistant, Annie.

"Certainly, Mr. Harrison," she said from their office in Cheyenne. Ten seconds later his cell phone rang.

"Mr. Clement," he told his director, "we have a problem."

It turned out Bill was already in town. Even better, he didn't seem to mind changing his schedule to accommodate Harrison's Boots—not surprising, given the amount of money they'd paid the man. The camera crew was a bit trickier, but money always helped to motivate people, and it worked in this instance, too. Like the director, they'd chosen to fly in the day before the shoot, which, given their tight parameters wasn't all that surprising. Once their flight landed, Annie got ahold of them and set everything up.

They were in business.

Ty tried to alert Ms. Sheppard via her cell phone. No answer. He wondered if she'd decided to ignore him—again. If so, she'd have a rude awakening. Left with no other choice, he went in search of her, walking up and down the rows of stalls. No luck. Next he tried the indoor arena, but she wasn't there, either. When he finally located her, standing alongside her horse trailer, his blood pressure had hit an all-time high.

"Why aren't you answering your cell?" he snapped, startling her, by the looks of it. She held a rope attached to her horse's halter. A man squatted near the back end of the animal, one of its rear legs in his lap.

"My cell phone?" she asked, pulling the thing from her pocket. "It hasn't even rung."

"Maybe it would if you turned it on," Ty said curtly.

"It *is* on," she retorted. Ty recognized the combative look in her gray eyes.

He could see she was right. The phone might be closed, but the digital display showed it was powered up.

He took the phone from her. "Well then, why—"

"Hey!" She tried to snatch it back.

"No bars," he said, after flipping the thing open. "Oops."

"Is there a problem?" The man working on her horse straightened. Worn chaps covered the front of his legs, and he held a rasp in one hand.

"No," Caroline said quickly. "Mr. Harrison here was just being his typical, high-handed self."

"Excuse me," Ty said, shocked that she would talk to him that way.

"It's true," she said, raising her chin. "But since you're here, I can only assume we're a go for the commercial."

"We are," he said, scanning her up and down—the T-shirt tucked into her jeans, the sparkling belt accentuating her narrow waist. Yes, under other circumstances he would have enjoyed bringing her to heel. "And since it took me nearly half an hour to find you, you now have less than an hour."

"I don't need an hour. I don't even need five minutes. I can wash up inside my trailer," she said, pointing at the rig, which, Ty noticed, was some sort of RV-horse trailer combination, complete with motor-home-type tinted windows near the front.

"I've arranged for a local makeup artist to assist you."

"I'd rather do my own."

He felt his blood begin to pound again. "Caroline, I know you're less than thrilled about our change of schedule, but it'll make it easier on everyone—myself included—if you'd just go with the flow."

He could tell she wanted to protest, but something held her back. Probably his subtle reminder that he was her sponsor.

"Dale, can we finish up later?" she asked.

"Sure. I was just filing the hoof around the new shoe. I can do that on my own."

Caroline sighed. "All right. Gimme a sec."

But she didn't seem in a big hurry to tie her horse

to the side of the trailer. And she took more than five minutes to wash her face—or whatever it was she did inside her trailer.

Brush her hair, he realized when she returned. Her most stunning attribute, he noted objectively, it looked like a collection of silk threads, each a different color, the whole mass so thick he'd have thought it fake if he didn't know better.

"Let's go," he said.

"Lead the way."

He turned, but not before noticing that she wiped her palms on the front of her jeans. When she tucked a strand of hair behind her ear, her hands shook.

"Caroline," he said, stopping abruptly. "There's no need to be nervous."

"What makes you think I'm nervous?"

"Aren't you?"

She took a deep breath, relaxed her shoulders and said, "All right. I'll admit it. I'm terrified."

"There's no need to be. The thing about filming a commercial is that we can do it again, if we need to."

"Yeah, but everyone has their limits. Your director won't be happy if I keep messing up, and neither, I suspect, will you."

"I won't mind."

"You'll mind if we end up having to reshoot the whole commercial. I imagine this is costing you a pretty penny."

No more so than *she'd* cost him. "We'll cross that bridge if we come to it."

He saw her swallow. "It's not just flubbing it that I'm worried about."

"It's not?"

She tugged her T-shirt down. "This is big. Once the commercial starts airing, my life will change. I know. I've seen it before. One of the bull riders got a big sponsorship deal. He started filming commercials, too, for some rental car agency. Suddenly he was being stopped for autographs, girls were calling out his name, people were writing him letters. He had to hire an assistant to deal with it all. I don't have *time* to hire an assistant."

"Harrison's Boots can handle the fallout, Caroline. You just concentrate on winning the NFR."

"Caro," she said. "Only my mom calls me Caroline."

He nodded. "And besides, I have a feeling you'll take to stardom well."

Stardom. When he said the word he saw her wince. "All I want to do is ride my horses, not sign autographs or do public appearances." She brushed a hand through her hair, the long strands catching in her fingers. "Maybe this was a mistake."

"You want to pull out?"

She looked him square in the eye. "What would you do if I said yes?"

He'd like to tell her hell no, they had way too

much money invested in her to allow that. Then he'd tell her to call an attorney.

But he wouldn't. He wasn't an insensitive ass, as much as she might think otherwise. It was apparent by the way she braced herself that that's exactly what she thought he'd tell her.

"If you're truly uncomfortable with this, you don't have to do it." Ty placed his hand on her shoulder and immediately felt her stiffen. Her cheeks filled with color. Her eyes ducked away from his.

"Thank you," she said to the ground.

He pulled his hand away. "You're welcome," he said softly.

A horse neighed in the distance. Ty could hear voices on the other side of one of the trailers.

"Let's go," she said, still not looking him in the eye.

Yes, they probably should go. Another moment and he might... *What?* Just what did he *think* he'd do?

Nothing, he reassured himself.

Chapter Four

Contrary to her belief that she'd muff it, Caroline could tell from the moment she said her first line that she'd been worried about nothing. Talking to the camera seemed as natural to her as riding a horse, maybe more so. She was able to smile, walk and talk, all at the same time, and without stumbling or bumping into the power cords and coaxial cables that hooked everything together.

And the whole time, Ty watched her, just as he had that first day, and she had no idea why that bothered her so much.

Afterward, Caro had a pounding headache. But she had to admit the commercial looked great. So authentic it seemed surreal—as if she really had walked her horse along a snowy lane.

"Caroline, that was fabulous," Bill, the director said, coming out from behind the camera after they'd filmed her saying her line "Harrison's Boots...the footwear of champions," from the back of Thumper. "If you ever want to change vocations and become an actress, I know an agent who'd be thrilled to have you."

"No thanks," she replied. That was the last thing she needed—a second career. She already had her hands full riding the rodeo circuit.

"Now that we're done with the vocals, I'd like to get some shots of you riding," Bill said.

Caro nodded, feeling Ty's eyes on her yet again as she led her horse toward the arena. He sat on the perimeter of the set in a dark green director's chair, sunglasses on and the sleeves of his white dress shirt rolled up. The black belt around his dark gray slacks accentuated his toned stomach.

Good-looking. Go ahead. Admit it again, she told herself. But remember what happened the *last* time your head was turned by a handsome man. *David.* She only had to think his name to have all the same emotions come flooding back. Regret. Sadness. Humiliation. *Never again.*

"Come on, Thumper," she said, happy to go for a ride. Grasping the leather reins, so worn and supple they felt like satin ribbons, she swung up into the saddle.

They'd attracted a crowd, she noticed once she mounted. People sat in chairs around the nearby stalls, watching the proceedings.

"Go, Caro," someone yelled, probably Mike. She could see his wide shoulders and big grin from a mile away.

"Just get on and ride around," Bill called through a bullhorn.

The scaffolding outside the arena didn't thrill Thumper at first, but Caro soothed him, looking up and catching Ty's gaze again. Damn it. Why did she keep doing that? She was like a stickpin near a magnet.

She kicked her horse forward. Someone yelled, "Yee-haw!" Probably Mike again. She felt self-conscious and silly. With a thick coat of makeup on her face and a fancy silver saddle on her horse—she had no idea where they'd gotten *that* from—she didn't feel like a barrel racer, but a freak.

"Okay, we've got a good camera angle here," Bill said, perched with his cameraman on one of the towers they'd erected. The long lens followed her faithfully. "If you could run now, that'd be great. Pretend you're headed toward one of those things you run around."

Barrel. It was called a barrel. But she did as asked, pressing her calves against Thumper. Her horse responded by lowering his neck and stretching out. Faster and faster they flew, the wind catching her hair and whipping it back, and soon she forgot everything. There was no camera, no audience, no Ty…just her and her horse and the rush of air against her face.

"Cut," Bill called, bringing Caro back to reality. Her headache also came crashing back.

A few people applauded. Caro pulled Thumper

up, her temples pounding with every beat of her heart. It was all she could do to slip off without throwing up.

"Nice," Ty said, appearing suddenly by her side.

"Thanks," she said.

"I think we can call it a day."

"Good," she breathed, resisting the urge to rub her forehead.

He stepped in front of her, forcing her gaze up. "You okay?" he asked softly.

And there it was again, that look in his eyes, the same one she'd noticed out by the trailers. Concern mixed with compassion.

"Fine," she said, walking Thumper forward. "Did we get everything done? Or will we have to shoot some more tomorrow?"

"I think we got it all," he said, walking beside her. Thumper's sides were expanding and contracting, after his impromptu workout. She'd have to cool him off.

"When will we know?" she asked, glancing over at the snow-covered ground. Rice flakes. Who'd have thought?

"Bill will review what we've got tonight. If it's okay, he'll let me know."

She nodded, her head throbbing even more. She winced.

"You're not all right, are you?"

"Just hungry," she said.

"You have any lunch?"

"No time."

He didn't look pleased. She was about to tell him to let it go, that she missed meals all the time. Part of life on the road. Fast food made you fat, and there was little or no time to cook. But Ty cut her off before she could open her mouth.

"Bill, we're going to Ms. Sheppard's trailer," he called.

"What's the matter?" The director peered into a monitor, reviewing the tape he'd just recorded.

"Caro needs an aspirin."

"I don't need medication," she said, stepping aside. "I need to cool off my horse."

"Don't give me that," he said. "I can tell you're in pain."

"I'm fine."

"You need to sit down," Ty said when she tried to get away.

"*You're* the one giving me a headache."

And a truer statement had never been uttered.

He frowned. "My mother had migraines, and I can tell yours is bad."

"It's not a migraine," Caro said. Thumper stopped abruptly, pulling her arm back and further jarring her head. She gasped.

"Migraine," Ty repeated.

"It's just stress. My head feels this way after I compete, too. Once an event is over, my temples start to throb."

"You're going back to your trailer."

"Ty—"

"No arguing, Caroline," he said, taking her by the arm again. "You need to sit down."

"Fine. But after I take something, I'm cooling down my horse."

"I'll do that for you."

"You don't know anything about horses."

"Actually, I do. I grew up on a ranch."

Caro was shocked, her eyes scanning his in an effort to discover if he was telling her the truth. For the first time she noticed how tanned he was. And that he appeared in excellent condition, his biceps straining against his dress shirt. She glanced at his hands.

They were a worker's hands, long and strong, with fine hairs bleached by the sun, and calluses mixed with tiny scars.

"You grew up on a ranch?"

"The Rocking H," he said. "We raise Herefords. Or my dad does. I haven't had much time to do anything since taking over the reins of Harrison's Boots, but I still get back there from time to time."

She felt her jaw begin to drop. She snapped it closed before she looked like a complete idiot. How had she not known this? Why hadn't anybody told her?

Why *would* someone tell her?

Harrison's Boots was a household name, just as a certain type of bread was well known, or a particular brand of TV. But she knew nothing about the long-time owners of the company. And their commercials offered no clues. Until now they'd featured big, burly men holding jackhammers or climbing skyscrapers, not riding horses. But now that she stepped back and looked at him—really looked— she recognized the signs of someone who spent a great deal of time out-of-doors.

The CEO was a cowboy.

"Come on," he said, obviously misinterpreting her silence for acquiescence. "Let's go."

Actually, now she really *did* need to sit down.

They made it to her trailer, Caro silent the whole time. "Go on inside," he said, taking Thumper's reins. "Sit down. As soon as I've unsaddled your horse, I'll be back."

"No," she said, having regained some of her composure. "Thumper needs to be walked. And you don't know where his stall is. It'd be better if I did it myself."

"Then tell me where to get the aspirin."

"It's in the medicine cabinet, in the bathroom," she said, wincing as she reached to loosen the girth.

Bong. Bong. Bong.

Her head felt like a Chinese gong whenever she bent down.

"Here," he said a moment later, bounding down the aluminum steps of her trailer. He held out two white tables and a bottle of water.

"Thanks."

"Where's your saddle go?"

She was in way too much of a hurry to swallow the pills to protest. "In the tack room," she rasped, the bitter taste of the painkiller filling her mouth. "Back of the trailer," she added after she'd gulped them down.

But she kept an eye on him as he picked up where she'd left off, expertly looping the billet strap around a metal ring so it wouldn't drag on the ground. Next he hooked the buckle at the end of the girth onto the leather strap attached to the side of the saddle. When he lifted the saddle off Thumper's back, pad and all, she finally looked away. She'd seen enough. He really *did* know something about horses.

"I'll be right back," he said.

"You don't need to walk him for too long," she said. Thumper's hooves clip-clopped against the pavement. "He hardly broke a sweat."

"Do you want me to cover his back?"

She was certain Ty must have seen the surprise in her eyes. A cold back might mean muscle spasms. "If you don't mind," she said. "There's a wool cooler in the trailer. Green."

He nodded before setting off. Caro slumped down on the steps, resting her head against the aluminum door. If she sat for a few minutes, she'd feel better. That's the way it always was.

I grew up on a ranch.

It'd been fine to think he was handsome when he

wasn't her type—busy, bossy corporate execs weren't her thing—but now she knew otherwise. He might not know anything about rodeos, but that wasn't because he came from the city. Obviously, he just didn't follow the sport. Until now. Until *her.*

Why did that make her feel odder still? She'd seen the hint of interest in his green eyes that first night. Was that part of the reason he'd agreed to sponsor her? Had his interest in her started *before* he'd met her?

And maybe your headache's made you crazy!

"Feeling better?" he asked a few minutes later.

Caro's head snapped up. Damn. He'd sneaked up on her.

"Uh, yeah," she said. "I think." She tried to move, tentatively at first, then slowly stood.

He'd been in the midst of coiling the lead rope, but stopped, one eyebrow lifted.

"Getting there," she amended.

"Good." His gaze lingering on her lips, and she froze.

Oh, no. No. No. No. You are not interested in him merely because you've learned he's a cowboy. Cowboys are clowns, remember? Cowboys are to be avoided at all costs.

Remember David?

"Um, thanks," she said. "But I should get to work."

"About that," he said, his mouth tipping into a slight smile.

Oh my.

Ty Harrison with a smile turned the three-alarm bells clanging in her head into an air-raid siren.

"I was thinking while walking old Thumper here," he said, patting the horse's neck. "What if I make you dinner?"

She was so busy trying to recover from that smile she found herself saying, "Huh?"

"I have a rental car. I can go out and get some steaks. You have an oven in there, I noticed. Why don't I broil some up?"

"You want to *make* me dinner."

"Yeah," he said. The smile dissolved like salt in vinegar. "Why are you looking at me like that?"

"Mr. Harrison, I—"

"Ty," he corrected.

Didn't he see? He couldn't be "Ty." He could never be, not to her.

"Mr. Harrison," she said, hoping he'd get the point. "That's really kind of you, but I'm busy—"

"You need to eat."

"I know. And I'll grab something. Just not right now."

"Actually," he said, "I'm not giving you a choice, not when I need you hale and hearty for the NFR." He held out Thumper's lead rope. "I'll have dinner ready by seven."

Chapter Five

To be honest, Ty half expected her trailer door to be locked when he got back. It was.

He smirked. Smart girl.

But he had her outwitted. Among his groceries was one lightweight, ultramodern, genuine hibachi. Hah. He also had briquettes, lighter fluid and barbecue tongs. As side dishes he'd bought potato salad and mixed greens. There were even late-season cobs of corn that he'd wrap in foil and grill. Everything he needed.

The sun had long since sunk beneath the horizon, but parking lights illuminated his cooking area at the back of the trailer. One of Caro's neighbors—a broad-shouldered man—took one look at Ty's groceries on the ground and said, "You need to borrow a table?"

"If you've got one handy," Ty replied, the flames from the hibachi licking the air and painting the side of the trailer a Halloween orange.

"Got one right here."

"Thanks."

"You cooking for Caro?" he asked when he returned, hauling a small folding table.

"I think so. I told her I would, but she didn't seem too enthusiastic."

"Let me guess," the man said, unfolding the table legs. "She told you not to bother."

"Actually, she locked her trailer door. If I hadn't bought the barbecue, I'd be stuck."

"That's Caro for you. Thinks she doesn't need a man, or that we're pretty useless." He set the table upright. "Mike Krueger," he said, holding out his hand.

"Ty Harrison."

"I know. Watched you film that commercial. Interesting stuff. Caro looked like she did great. 'Course, you could film Caro upside down, walking on her hands, and she'd look gorgeous."

"That's certainly true," Ty said, arranging his groceries on the table. "You don't happen to have a salad bowl, do you?"

"Got everything you need," Mike said, motioning toward his own long, white trailer. The lights were on inside and Ty could see a TV flickering behind the windows. Modern day cowboys. "Just help yourself."

"Are you leaving?" Ty asked when Mike turned away.

"Yup. I was about to close things up. I'm in the

main performance. But I can leave it open in case you need something else."

"That'd be much appreciated."

"And before I go, think I'll find Caro and tell her she has a guest."

Ty smiled. "You do that."

She showed up fifteen minutes later. By then Ty had the steaks on, and the smell of sizzling meat filled the air.

"What do you think you're doing?"

"Cooking," he said without looking up. "Like I told you."

She didn't say anything. Ty risked a peek. *Furious* didn't begin to describe the expression on her face.

"Whatever," she said, walking back toward the barn.

He let the steaks continue to cook. "Caro, wait." She sped up. He was faster. "Don't leave. Not without eating first. If you want to ignore me the whole time, fine. But at least get some food in your stomach."

The light from Mike's trailer perfectly illuminated her face. She seemed exhausted. Near the corners of her eyes, the skin appeared bruised, something you wouldn't notice unless you were staring at her closely.

"How long has it been since you've had a home-cooked meal, anyway?"

The steaks suddenly hissed, as if punctuating his remark. She gritted her teeth. She'd changed since the shoot, the pressed cotton shirt she'd worn replaced by another T-shirt, which read I'm Going to Treat You Like My Dog, Cowboy.

You Wish!

Well, now he knew her treatment of him was nothing personal.

"Months?" He hazarded a guess.

She shrugged. "Can't remember."

"Do you ever slow down, Caroline?"

"I told you. Only my mom calls me Caroline," she reminded him. "And, yes, I do slow down. When the season's over. Until then I can't afford to take it easy."

"Will having one little steak hurt you?"

She raised her chin, her gray eyes managing to look even bigger in the murky half-light. "I'm behind today."

Thanks to filming a commercial. She didn't say it, but might as well have.

"Then take the food with you. I've got paper plates. Stop and eat."

She slowly nodded. Ty wondered if she'd toss the plate away the moment he was out of sight.

"Have a seat," he said. "The steaks need to cook for a few more minutes."

She crossed her arms, turned and then sat in one of the folding chairs Mike had let him borrow.

"If I had my way you wouldn't get up from that chair for at least an hour," he said, waving the barbecue tongs at her before squatting down and flipping the steaks.

"Then it's a good thing I don't have to listen to you."

He pulled out a chair, too, and took a seat. "Why are you fighting this?"

"Fighting what?"

"This," he said, leaning toward her.

Her gray eyes widened.

She thought he was about to kiss her. He could tell by the way she drew back, her chest expanding, and then didn't move as she waited…

But he wasn't going to kiss her. He had no intention of ever crossing the line with her. He grabbed the salad bowl.

"My desire to feed you," he said, keeping his expression carefully blank, because he couldn't deny they were obviously attracted to each other.

"I don't mind you feeding me," she said after expelling a breath. "I mean…" She ran a hand through her hair. "All right, maybe I do."

"You need to take better care of yourself, slow down a little," he said, trying to steer the conversation to neutral ground. His heart pounded in an odd way. "I don't want a comatose spokesperson."

"I can't slow down. This is how I make my living."

"I lead a busy life, too," he said, shifting on the plastic seat. "But I still take it easy from time to time."

"What you and I do are completely different things," she said.

"Not really," he said. "We both have vocations we're completely dedicated to. Granted, riding a horse is different than selling boots, but *I* have the added pressure of working for a family business. One that I took over at a young age."

He got up, checked on the steaks, flipping them over again and sending smoke rising in the air.

Ty shrugged. "My father never wanted to be involved. He likes to call himself a cowboy, not a corporate executive. It was patently obvious, even when I was a child, that I would be the next Harrison to carry on the family business—the sooner, the better."

"And you resisted?"

"No. I happen to enjoy the thrill of competition. Running Harrison's is a constant challenge."

"I imagine so."

"My dad prefers raising cattle."

"What about you?" Caro asked. "Do you like living on a ranch?"

"I used to love it," he said. "Before…"

"Before what?" she prompted.

"My mom died."

He poked at the steaks, ostensibly to check if they were done. The subject of his mom's death was obviously painful.

Caro knew just how he felt. People still asked about her own father. If they didn't know he'd passed away, she was left with the task of breaking the news. And if they'd heard he'd died, she was forced to put on a brave face and say everything was fine. But it wasn't fine. She still missed him. Had ridden her heart out for him this past year. If she made it to the NFR, she'd be doing it in his honor.

If she made it.

She watched absently as Ty took the steaks off the fire. The meat hissed and sputtered, the smell of perfectly cooked fillets filling the air.

"How did she die?" Caro murmured. "If you don't mind me asking."

He put some salad greens on her plate, then popped the lid of something else—a tub of potato salad, she realized, watching as he scooped some on, as well. Her stomach growled.

"Flu."

"Flu?" she repeated, surprised.

"It happens," he said. "Far more often than you realize. And my mom was always frail, so that didn't help. We suspect the medication she took for her headaches weakened her immune system somehow, but there's no way to prove it."

"I'm sorry," she said softly. "I lost my dad last year."

Ty met her gaze, the fork he'd been using to stab at the rib eyes suddenly still. "I had no idea."

"He's the reason I'm doing this." She splayed her hands, indicating the rodeo grounds.

He set the plate of food down. "How so?"

She absently traced the edge of the table with a finger. "I was planning on being a vet. Like my brother. I'd completed my B.A., was ready to start on my upper grad work, when my mom called to say dad wasn't feeling well. Before he left for the hospital he told me not to worry, that everything would be okay. I didn't realize it then, but that was the last time I would talk to him."

Caro looked Ty in the eye. "He had a heart attack in the hospital."

"Oh man…" He shook his head.

"I didn't even have time to get there. I was out in the Bay Area, and drove like a madwoman the whole way home, because if my dad was saying he didn't feel well, I knew something was seriously wrong. My mom knew it, too. I could hear the panic in her voice."

It was the first time she'd talked about this to anyone, Caro realized, and she had no idea why she was finally opening up with Ty. Except, maybe she did. He'd been through it, too, and so he understood. Only someone who'd experienced the death of a loved one knew what it was like to miss someone to the point that it became a physical pain. Knew what it was like to dread the upcoming holidays, to set a place at a Thanksgiving dinner table when you *knew* no one would be sitting there. Caro felt tears come to her eyes as she admitted to herself that some of the stress she felt—the overwhelming, sometimes nearly unbearable strain—was because of her father's death. She hated competing with him not around.

"He died just before I got there. The man who told

me I could be anything I wanted to be, who supported me no matter what mistakes I made, who loved me no matter how stupidly I behaved…that man was gone."

"I'm really sorry," Ty said quietly.

She inhaled deeply. "During the funeral, I decided to try for the National Finals. He'd always encouraged me to do that. Told me time and again I was as good, if not better, than the girls who ran the circuit full-time. I thought I might have a shot at it, too, because once before I'd been primed to do it, but I got…distracted. This time I'm not letting anyone or anything get in my way."

Including you.

"You've done remarkably well, given everything you're coping with."

"You're right. I'm almost there."

He placed a hand on her knee. She straightened, thinking for a moment that he might…

But he didn't.

"I'm sorry," he said once more, his hand resting on her leg.

The steaks were forgotten. So was qualifying for the NFR.

"I can tell you're still grieving," he said.

"I am. It's been over a year, but I still miss him."

"You'll always miss him."

"I know," she said, drawing back. "And *you* know, too."

"I do," he said solemnly.

Something changed. Caro couldn't move. He seemed to grow still, too.

"I should go," she said, scooping up the plate. "I want to watch the other girls compete in tonight's main performance. I'll eat in the stands."

"Caro," Ty said, standing with her. "If you ever need someone to talk to..."

He'd be there for her. She could see it in his eyes. She might not know him all that well, but she could sense his compassion.

"Thanks," she said, turning.

She thought he might follow. Thought he might offer to sit in the grandstands with her.

Do you want him to sit with you, Caro?

She did. And that was all the more reason to get away, fast. She could feel herself slipping, and that would never do. Once before a man had cost her the NFR. Never again.

Never.

Chapter Six

When she got back to her trailer later that night, he was gone. A good thing, she quickly told herself. Ty Harrison would remain a professional acquaintance, that was all.

If you ever need to talk...

But she could never call him. Best to keep that invisible line drawn in the sand. Sponsor, spokesperson. That's what they were to each other. That's all they'd ever be.

But the next morning he was back.

She was in the midst of hosing off Classy at the rear of her trailer when he appeared. Caro didn't see him at first—she was bent over, busily rinsing the mare's legs. Her second-string barrel horse was covered with sweat, so warm that steam rose from the animal's back.

"I brought you breakfast."

Caro jumped. The hose she held came along with

her. A stream of water hit Classy in the belly, causing the mare to flick her head up in protest.

"Sorry," she told the animal, turning on Ty next. "Mr. Harrison. What are you doing here?"

The formal use of his name was a blatant reminder. Sponsor, spokesperson. Or so she hoped. But she could tell he wasn't pleased about the return to formality.

He held up a bag.

"I don't eat that stuff," she said, turning back to her mare, water slashing against the asphalt and dotting her leather boots—Harrison's, of course. The water came from her own storage tank, and she didn't want it to go to waste, so continued with her task. If Mr. Harrison thought that was rude, too bad.

"It's eggs and a pancake. Surely that can't be bad for you."

"I never eat breakfast," she said, moving to the other side of her horse. There was no electric pump. The water pressure was practically nonexistent.

"Caro, what's wrong?" he asked.

She considered saying nothing was wrong. Or maybe pretending she didn't understand the question. But knowing what she did about Ty, he probably wouldn't fall for it. She shut off the water, wiping her hands on her jeans. "We need to talk."

"I'm right here."

Yes, he was, and downright sexy in his faded jeans and button-down beige shirt. He didn't need to wear a cowboy hat to look appealing. Something about his rugged features all but oozed masculinity. She couldn't believe she hadn't noticed it before.

She tossed the same wool cooler Ty had used on Thumper yesterday over Classy's back, then made sure the mare's lead rope was securely fastened to a metal ring on the outside of the trailer.

"I won't go out with you."

"Excuse me?"

She pulled her shoulders back and made sure she looked him square in the eyes. "I can tell that you're…" she searched for the right word "…interested in me. And I'm not going to lie. I feel something, too. But I'm the last person on earth you should get involved with, for many reasons."

It was early morning, but the sun was already shining against the side of the trailer, the light reflecting off it and illuminating his face. She could see emotion flicker in his eyes.

"You're wrong. My interest in you is purely professional."

"Then what are you doing here this morning?"

"Since your cell phone doesn't work, I came over to tell you that Bill considers the commercial in the can. You might have to do some in-studio vocal work next week, but that should be easy to fit into your schedule."

She felt her cheeks heat. That wasn't why he'd come to see her. She was certain of it.

"The breakfast was an attempt to keep you eating, but if you don't want food, so be it. I'll see you after you ride. That was the other reason I came out here this morning. I'd like to watch my investment ride."

His *investment?*

"I'll see you later," he said. "Ms. Sheppard."

He'd taken three steps when she found her voice. "Wait."

He turned back to her.

Caro didn't know what to think. He was either one smooth talker, or telling the truth. If the latter, she'd completely misjudged him. And was a prize idiot.

"I'm sorry, Mr. Harrison. Last night I thought—"

"That I was coming on to you?" he finished. "No, Caroline. I was just trying to be a friend. You looked like you needed one."

A friend.

She hadn't had one of those in years.

"Well, all right then," she said. "I guess I owe you an apology…for leaping to the wrong conclusion. And I should say thank-you, too, for dinner last night and now for breakfast."

"You're welcome," he said, giving her a cool, impersonal smile. "But since you don't want your eggs and pancakes, maybe you should give them to Mike. I have a feeling he'd take them."

"You're probably right."

"I'll see you after," Ty said.

"After," she said, watching him walk away.

* * *

"You going to kick my butt?" Melanie asked Caro a couple hours later. Melanie was one of her closest rodeo friends—if two fiercely competitive people could ever be friends. Most of the time they couldn't, Caro had learned.

They were warming up their horses, or at least that's what Caroline had been trying to do. She'd spotted Ty standing by the rail of the arena, and felt confused all over again.

What was it about that man?

He's only the most handsome man you've met in a long while. Rich. Powerful. A cowboy.

"Hello?" Melanie said. "Earth calling Caroline."

"I don't know," Caro replied at last, shoving her black hat down on her head. "I'm feeling off," she admitted.

"This doesn't have something to do with that handsome hunk of a sponsor you scored yourself, does it?"

"What?"

"Everyone's talking about him. We're hoping he decides to sponsor *two* barrel racers next year."

"You're kidding."

"*You* must be kidding if you hadn't noticed what a hunk he is."

"Actually, I hadn't."

Liar, liar, liar.

"We were all wondering who he was when you were filming that commercial yesterday," Melanie said, her glittery blue shirt sparkling in the sun. The camera equipment was all gone, Caro noted. Only the scaffolding and a few lingering "snow drifts" remained. "Once we figured it out, there was just about a stampede in his direction. But he didn't leave your side. Lea told me that after she performs today, she's going to go up and introduce herself."

Caro glanced at Lea. The pretty barrel racer was warming her horse up, too, and every time she loped by Ty, she smiled at him.

"Well, I wish her luck."

"You mean you're *not* interested in him?" Melanie asked.

"You ought to know the answer to that."

Her friend tipped her head. "Still messed up over that, huh?"

"That" being Caro's college boyfriend, David, the one who'd claimed to love her. Melanie had competed on the college rodeo circuit, too, so she knew the story. Caro had fallen hard for a bull rider, hard enough that she'd contemplated marrying him. He'd promised her everything, and ended up breaking her heart.

"Not messed up," Caro said. "Just older and wiser."

"Too bad," Melanie said.

Yeah, too bad.

"Well, good luck today." The other rider's dark curls bounced against her back as she set off at a trot.

"Good luck," Caro replied, watching her with a sense of envy. Last weekend, that had been her. She'd been ready to run her pattern, anxiously awaiting her turn. Today she kept stealing glances at the arena fence, or more accurately, at Ty.

She'd lost her focus.

Damn it. She clucked to her horse, her hat knocked back a bit by the sudden movement. She shoved it down again, determined to trot past Ty as if she didn't know him. She succeeded, too, but only for a couple seconds at a time. Every time she passed him, she felt his eyes on her.

Concentrate.

But she couldn't, and she knew it, and so she had a bad feeling the moment her number was called. Thumper started to act up, too, the tension in her own muscles sending the gelding into a tailspin—literally.

"Damn it," she muttered, having to work to keep him facing the right direction.

"You're up as soon as 298's done," the gate man said. Terri Bruce was 298, Caro knew, because she'd watched the woman try to control her own horse. Maybe something was in the air. That happened sometimes.

But suddenly she wondered if she'd messed up somehow. If maybe she hadn't worked him enough. She hadn't even glanced at her watch to mark the time when she'd entered the warm-up arena. She'd been concentrating on other things.

Ty.

"Easy there, boy," she said, to no avail.

This is what you get for having your head in the clouds. You'll be lucky to stay on tonight.

"Come on, boy," she said softly, patting his neck. "Try to save that energy for when we're out there."

Inside, a few spectators erupted in cheers, urging Terri on. The Louisiana stadium was like many other indoor venues in that there wasn't a straight shot to the arena. It was another blind turn, this one to the right. She couldn't see what was going on, but as each successive cheer got louder, she could tell Terri was having an awesome run.

Terri was behind her in money earned. If she had a good night, it might bump Caro out of the running. Unless Terri had a bad run next weekend. But a few of the other girls would have to have an off night, too.

Caroline!

Thumper seemed to sense her distraction, tried to take advantage of it. He lurched forward, bucking.

"Whoa!" she ordered, one hand grabbing at her hat, which had been knocked askew.

He bucked again, his front leg so high off the ground, she caught sight of the pink leg wraps around his cannon bones.

"Thumper!"

Terri rounded the blind corner, still at an all-out run.

"Oh, shit."

Thumper must have had the same thought, because he planted all four feet, then danced to the right. Terri flew by.

"You're on," the gate man said.

Her horse lurched forward. Caro let him go and hung on.

But something wasn't right.

She could tell the moment he took his first running step. This was no smooth gait. And it was no flat-out run. Thumper seemed hesitant, almost tentative as he headed toward the arena.

Caro experienced everything in stark relief. Like one of those dreams where everything seems to tick off in reverse, she saw herself pull back, saw Thumper begin to slow.

But then he caught sight of the arena and didn't *want* to slow.

"Thumper," she cried again, though her lips seemed to move long before she heard the words.

He charged forward, muscles straining.

He'd spotted the first barrel.

She jerked back. He shook his head.

"Whoa!" she commanded, panicked now. Something was wrong. She could *feel* it. But in a flash they were at the first obstacle. She felt his shoulder tip, heard herself call, "Whoa."

Too late.

Thumper tried to turn, but something had to hurt him because he pulled up suddenly. Caro hung on. But gravity had hold of her now, and when Thumper's front leg buckled beneath him, they both tilted right.

She hit the ground hard.

Ty screamed her name.

He watched as Caro seemed to fly through the air, her horse nearly landing atop her.

"Son of a *bitch*."

The words came from somebody, he wasn't certain who. He was too busy leaping up from his front-row seat. He jumped over the arena railing. He wouldn't remember doing it later, and when he saw what a drop it was, he would marvel that he hadn't killed himself. His knees gave out when he landed, and he fell forward, damp earth squishing between his fingers. He didn't care. He was a hundred feet away and he could see Caro's horse straining to stand.

"Caroline!"

She hadn't moved.

Her horse lifted his head, then began to bob it up and down as he tried to stand. Ty recognized the signs. Caro was too close. If the paint lurched to his feet, he would step on her.

"Caroline!" Ty shouted.

She stirred. Her hand moved, knocking against her hat, which had landed nearby. But she didn't get up.

His heart jolted. Thumper stuck a leg out, perilously close to Caro's head.

"Caroline!"

She must have heard him. Or else it was just dumb luck that she rolled to the right.

The gelding stood, and staggered…left. Thank God.

Out of the corner of his eye Ty could see other people rushing toward her, too. Paramedics, their blue uniforms visible against the arena's beige walls. One of the rodeo workers, in a western shirt. Someone else on foot; one of the cowboys from behind the chutes, by the looks of it. Ty sank to his knees beside Caro as she sat up.

"Don't move," he ordered.

"What happened?"

"You fell."

"Do you remember what day it is?" the paramedic asked, a pimple-faced kid who couldn't be older than nineteen.

"I know I fell. And it's Saturday. And I meant, what happened to Thumper," she said, this time louder. "Something was wrong with him from the moment he started to gallop." She tried to stand.

"Stay still," the paramedic ordered. "Ms. Sheppard, we need you to lie down until we determine the extent of your injuries."

"I'm not injured," she said, moving her legs beneath her. "My *horse* is."

"Caroline," Ty said, sharper, "stay still."

Their gazes met. He saw her chin jut out. "Thumper's in pain," she said. "I could feel it in his gait."

"You might be injured, too," the cowboy said.

When Ty glanced up, he realized it was the rodeo clown. "And you won't do that horse of yours no good if you hurt yourself worse by getting up when you shouldn't."

The man's words were the only thing that seemed to get through to her, and she relaxed. Ty told himself it was ridiculous to feel put out by that. He didn't know Caroline well enough to expect her to listen to him.

"Someone stand by Thumper," she ordered.

"He isn't going anywhere," the rodeo worker announced.

"Lie back," the paramedic said at the same time.

The gelding stood there, one leg stretched out in front of him. Ty's stomach turned. That wasn't a good sign.

"Just the same, I want someone to go stand with my horse. If he's hurt, I don't want him running off."

The rodeo worker nodded, and then went and did as she asked. Ty heard the paramedic ask her what day it was again, what her name was, where they were. She answered all the questions easily, but her focus was on her horse.

She looked about ready to cry. Obviously she, too, knew the signs of equine distress. Head down. Sides heaving. Legs splayed. Thumper exhibited all the indications of an animal in severe pain.

"Damn it," she said. "I'm fine."

They let her rise. Ty bent and picked up her hat, which was covered with dirt. The people in the grandstands and behind the chutes cheered her on. Caroline lifted a hand absently, telling the spectators—mostly fellow rodeo performers, since she performed in slack—that she was all right. But she wasn't. Ty had to steady her when she took a step.

"Thumper," he heard her say softly. "Hey, boy."

The rodeo clown looked strangely pensive, despite the smile painted on his face. "Caro, I think he *is* in a lot of pain."

"I know," she said. Ty watched as she made quick work of removing the bright pink leg wrap. She ran her hand down Thumper's limb. "Son of a—" She stifled a sob.

"What?" another man asked. "What is it?"

Ty wondered who the tall, blond man was until Caroline said, "I think he's got a fracture, Doc."

The vet knelt by the horse's leg, running his hands up and down the cannon bone. He stopped for a second, gently probing an area on the front of Thumper's leg, right above the fetlock. The horse tried to jerk his leg away. "Yeah. I think you're right," he said, his Texas drawl clearly noticeable. "Damn."

"Do you want me to call for an equine ambulance, Dr. Lampkin?" the rodeo clown asked.

"Yeah. Louisiana State U has got one," the vet said, standing. "Call them. They're the ones best equipped to handle this type of injury anyway."

"What can we do to help with the pain?" Caro

said, her voice thick with tears. Ty could see she was working hard not to cry.

"I'll give him something to take the edge off," the jean-clad vet said, resting his hands on his hips. "But I don't want to give him too much, not if we're going to have to move him."

If. Because they might have to put Thumper down. Ty didn't need to hear the words to know that's what everyone was thinking.

"I'll go get my bags," Dr. Lampkin said. "And my laptop. It has ultrasound. I wanna see how bad that break is before we attempt anything. Walt, we're going to have a bit of a delay."

Ty glanced behind him. Walt Provo, the rodeo official he'd met yesterday, was nodding. "Whatever you need."

Caro turned her head away. Ty moved in next to her, murmuring, "We'll fix him up, Caro."

She didn't say anything and Ty knew she was thinking, *but what if we can't?*

"I've heard UC Davis is implanting screws in horses' legs now," Walt said. "One of our stock contractors had a bucking horse that broke a leg. That mare was back in the shoots a little over a year later."

Caro turned and faced them both. Ty had to clench his hands to keep from reaching out and touching her when he saw tears on her cheeks. "My brother graduated from UC Davis."

"Then maybe he knows someone to call over there," Walt said.

"I'm going to phone him."

"Use my cell," Ty said.

"Rand," he heard her say a few minutes later, and for a second Ty thought she might lose it. "Thumper's hurt."

Obviously, her brother asked what happened, because she told him everything, right up to her falling off. "Doc Lampkin thinks it's a fractured cannon bone." She was silent a moment before saying, "No. He went to get his bag. But he'll be back in a minute. Hold on. Here he comes right now."

Ty saw the vet jogging toward them, a syringe hanging out of his pocket and a square leather bag in his hand. His long, angular face gleamed with sweat.

"Doc," Caro said, "I have my brother on the phone. He's an alumni of UC Davis Veterinary School. Can I put him on speakerphone?"

Dr. Lampkin nodded. "Sure. Just let me get set up here."

The man squatted down. Inside the leather bag was a laptop, and Ty watched as the doctor powered it up, plugged something into it—a wand of some sort—and then said, "Okay, put him on."

Everyone stared at the phone Caroline held as Dr. Lampkin nodded. "I'm firing up the ultrasound right now, but based on swelling and the amount of pain the animal is in, I'd say we're dealing with a cannon bone fracture on the distal or lower end."

Ty glanced at Caro to see how she took the news. She was staring at the computer screen, her hand clutching a strand of Thumper's mane. The rodeo clown still held the lead rope. His eyes, too, were on the monitor. Dr. Lampkin picked up the wand. The black background faded to gray. Ty marveled at the simplicity of it all as the laptop became an equine diagnostic device.

"I'm probing the third metacarpal right now."

Ty held his breath. Caro likely did the same. The gray turned to white, Caro turning away for a second when she spotted the same thing everyone else no doubt did. Along the white line was an area of shadow, a lateral smudge even Ty could identify as a break.

"Yup. It's a condylar fracture."

Son of a—

"Now, Caroline," Ty heard her brother say through the speakerphone. "Don't you panic. U.C. Davis had a lot of success repairing this type of fracture. Dr. Danson there is one of the best in the business when it comes to fractures, and I'm sure he'd be happy to consult. That it's a condylar is actually *good* news. The important thing is to keep that leg isolated so Thumper doesn't do more damage. I'm sure Dr. Lampkin there knows how to handle that."

"I do. And we're going to take him to LSU," the vet said.

"Good. I'll get someone to cover my clinic, and I'll fly out as soon as I can."

"Oh, Rand," Caro said, fresh tears spilling. "You'd do that?"

"Of course," Ty heard him say. "Thumper's a member of the family. As sure as I am that Doc Lampkin knows what he's doing, I know you'll feel better if I'm there."

"I will," Caro said, her face pale beneath the arena lights, the hand that held the cell phone visibly shaking.

"You won't need to fly commercial," Ty said. "I have a private jet that can pick you up. Just tell me what airport is closest to you."

"Who's that?" he heard Rand ask.

"That's Ty Harrison," Caro said, wiping her face again. "He's my sponsor."

"A private jet, huh?" Rand asked.

"It can be there in a matter of hours."

"Well, if you don't mind spending the money for it to come pick me up, that'd sure save on time."

"Anything to help Caro out," Ty said, noticing that Caro's hand shook as she held the phone. "Maybe you can get Dr. Danson to come along, too."

When Ty glanced at Caro, he saw her face light up. "Do you think Dr. Danson would, Rand?"

"He might," Rand said. "If I promise him a case of wine."

"I'll buy him a whole vineyard, if that'll get him here," Ty said.

"You'll be in good hands if you can do that," Dr. Lampkin said. "I've heard good things about Dr. Danson."

"I can't promise he'll come," Rand said. "But I have a feeling he will, especially when I tell him it's for my sis's horse."

"Thanks, Rand," Caro said, clearing her throat. "I'll be in touch."

Chapter Seven

Rand called back less than five minutes later. Caro felt a burst of hope when he told her Dr. Danson would be coming with him.

"Excellent," Dr. Lampkin said. "Now let's see what we can do to get Thumper more comfortable."

Mike appeared by her side, and Caro buried herself in his arms.

"You doin' okay?" the big cowboy asked.

"I'll be doing better once we move Thumper."

Mike nodded.

What followed was an excruciating hour of waiting for the drugs to take affect, then for the temporary cast Dr. Lampkin set around Thumper's leg to harden and the equine ambulance to arrive. But the worst part was the self-blame.

Why hadn't she pulled Thumper up? She'd known something was wrong the moment he'd taken that first step. And before that. Why hadn't she been more careful warming him up? She should have worked him for at least another half hour. But she hadn't, because she'd been distracted.

Ty.

She glanced over at him. They were in his car, following the equine ambulance. She'd wanted to ride with her horse, but Doc Lampkin had been dead set against it. LSU had sent a team along to help Thumper in the trailer. They didn't need her.

Broken leg.

She tried not to cry, turning her head to look out the passenger window so Ty wouldn't see her break down.

No NFR.

But that didn't matter, she told herself. Nothing mattered but getting Thumper well. Because this was *her* fault. If she hadn't been so damn distracted...

"You okay?" Ty asked.

She couldn't look at him. If she did, she might do something stupid, like lash out—which would be really childish, because he hadn't been the one to mess up.

"I'm fine," she lied.

"We'll get him fixed up, Caro. I promise."

Would they? And if they didn't, what then? Should she ride in next week's rodeo? On one of her backup horses?

No. She couldn't do that. Her heart wouldn't be in it.

* * *

"All right, let's be careful unloading him," Doc Lampkin said when they arrived less than an hour later.

LSU's pristine veterinary clinic was a single-story structure that resembled UC Davis's teaching facilities: a massive barn, with horizontal bars across the fronts of the stalls, and rubber mats on the floors. She'd visited her brother on campus only a few times, but the diagnostic area looked the same. Large whitewashed rooms were filled with state-of-the-art equipment.

"This way to X-ray," one of the assistants said.

Thumper was still drugged, his neck slick with sweat. His steps were slow, and every time he put weight on his injured leg, he stopped and had to be coaxed forward. Caro hated that he had to walk, but there was no other way to get him inside. Loading him in the trailer had been painful to watch, too.

"Should I follow?" she asked, not knowing what to do or where to go, now that they were here.

"Of course," the vet tech, a pretty blonde with a reassuring smile, said.

"Do you want me to come along?" Ty asked Caro.

"That's up to you," she replied, knowing she sounded curt, but unable to stop her self-loathing from leaching into her words.

No one to blame but herself.

"We can always use an extra set of hands," the petite blonde said.

"Who's the lead vet here?" Dr. Lampkin asked, his gaze never leaving Thumper.

"That'd be Dr. Merrill. He's going to meet us in X-ray."

X-rays only confirmed Dr. Lampkin's diagnosis. So did nuclear imaging. By the time three hours had passed, Caroline knew the exact length, location and type of break Thumper had. The good news was that all three vets on the case agreed Thumper's prognosis was excellent. The bad news was that Rand and Dr. Danson wouldn't be able to fly in until the next day, because Danson had to perform a surgery on another horse. But the LSU vets informed her that waiting until the next day wouldn't hurt Thumper's chances for recovery. They just had to operate within the first forty-two hours.

"Give us the name of your hotel," Dr. Halloway, one of the attending veterinarians, said.

"We're staying at the Marriott." When Ty caught Caro's look of surprise, he added, "I had my assistant book us rooms."

Because they needed to stay someplace while they operated on her horse.

The horse she was supposed to have ridden in the NFR. Thumper—her high school rodeo horse, an animal who'd taken her almost to the top—ruined. Maybe forever.

"The Marriott. Got it," the doctor said. "We'll see you in the morning then."

She nodded, taking deep breaths to keep the tears at bay. "I'll be here, but before I go, can I say good-bye to Thumper?"

"Of course," the vet said. "You know where he's at."

She did. Strapped to a harness in a rubber-padded stall, an IV hanging out of his neck. Caro walked blindly into the barn, breathing faster and faster as she fought the urge to bow her head and sob.

"Thumper," she called softly to the half-drugged animal. She felt her heart lurch when he tried to lift his head, his ears pricking forward. "Oh, Thumper," she said, moving slowly into his stall. Billet straps around his abdomen kept him suspended in the center of the space. The stark-white cast seemed to glow in the barn's fluorescent lighting. "Hey there, boy," she said, patting his neck.

Once again he tried to lift his head, but it was simply too much for him.

"You okay?" she heard Ty ask as she stroked his neck.

No. I'm not okay, she wanted to scream. *I'm very definitely not okay.*

"Fine," she said. "We'll get him all fixed up, won't we, Thumper, old boy."

She rested her head against his neck, feeling his soft hair against her cheek, and suddenly it was all too much. Thumper had been part of her life for nearly ten years. She'd gotten him when she was a teenager—

a gift from her father—and had ridden him up through the ranks to becoming a professional. She'd won her first rodeo on him, and been voted Los Molinos Rodeo Queen from his back. He was her partner on the rodeo circuit, but most of all he was her friend.

"Caroline, shh…" Ty whispered, taking her into his arms. She told herself not to let him, but she was too weak to resist the offer of a warm shoulder to cry on.

"I don't know what I'll do if I have to put him down."

"You won't have to put him down," he said.

"I might, Ty." Caro drew back from him. "I need to be honest with myself. If the surgery tomorrow doesn't go well, if the anesthesia affects him the wrong way or he struggles, or thrashes around when they start to wake him up… I just don't think I can stand to lose him. Not after everything that happened to us, getting to this point."

"What do you mean?" Ty asked.

She debated how much to tell him, but she was too far sunk in her own misery to care if he knew it all. "I tried to qualify for the NFR once before."

"You did?"

"I would have made it, too. Thumper and I were smoking that year. Nobody could touch us. It got so bad people would drop out when they saw my truck and trailer pull into the rodeo grounds."

"What happened?"

"I met a man." She could tell she'd shocked him, but blindly forged on. "I was young and stupid. Thought I knew better than anyone else. My friends warned me to stay away. David was trouble, they said. A bull rider so hung up on himself that in hindsight I'm surprised his head could fit between the chutes. But I fell for him, hard. And for a while it was okay. It was fun having a boyfriend who rode the circuit, too. But then rumors started finding their way back to me. If I wasn't with David at a rodeo, I heard other women were. I didn't want to believe it. When I confronted him, of course he denied it. Told me he loved me and that he wanted to marry me. We'd be the dynamic duo of the rodeo circuit, and I almost fell for it."

"Was he cheating?"

"He had girlfriends in every state, but what made it all the more humiliating was that they all knew about me. He'd told them we had an open relationship, that he was allowed to see whoever he wanted, and they all bought it. One of the girls was a barrel racer out of Oklahoma. She took great delight in telling me all the sordid details."

"You must have been devastated."

"I gave up rodeo." Caro crossed her arms in front of her. "I couldn't face him. Couldn't face all those girls. So I quit." She looked Ty in the eye. "Biggest mistake of my life."

She turned back to Thumper, smoothed his mane

down, ran her hands along his neck. "He became my trail horse," she said. "I went to work on my parents' dude ranch. Everyone thought I was crazy, quitting like that. But I think the person I most disappointed was my dad."

She heard Ty come up to her, felt his hand on her shoulder. "I know just how you feel."

"Do you?" she asked absently, her heart constricting all over again when Thumper tried to turn to her. The IV drip that hung around his head swiveled with him on its supporting arm.

"When I first graduated college I decided to find a job outside of the family business."

"You did?" she asked, more out of politeness than anything else.

"I thought my father wouldn't care. He'd never shown any interest in running the family business. My grandfather did most of the work while he was alive. When he died my senior year of college, I thought we should sell the company. My going to work outside the industry was in preparation for that, but when I told my father, he hit the roof."

Caro turned to face Ty, one of her hands still on Thumper's neck.

"It turns out my father and grandfather had always planned for me to run Harrison's. It wasn't that my father didn't want the business, just that he knew I'd be better with it. He's proud of Harrison's Boots, proud of his heritage, and I'd never seen him more upset than when I told him I thought we should sell."

"I told my dad I thought I should sell Thumper."

"And what did he say?"

"That one day I'd realize no man was worth the loss of a dream. Only here I am again, my chances ruined because of a man."

"What do you mean?" Ty asked.

"I couldn't focus this morning…because of *you*."

He took a step back. "What?"

"I'm attracted to you, Ty. And you're attracted to me, too, don't deny it. I saw it in your eyes."

She watched him tense for a moment before he drew himself up. "Very well, I won't deny it," he said softly. "I've wanted you from the moment I first set eyes on you."

She felt her body flush, felt a rush of pleasure spread to places that hadn't been touched in a long, long time. And that still wouldn't be touched.

"It would never work."

"Yes, Caroline, it would."

"No, it wouldn't."

"Why not?"

She lifted her chin. "Because one day I'll make another play for the NFR. It'll be a long shot, especially on a young horse, but I have to try. If not for my sake, then for my father, who always believed I could do it."

"And you're going to live like a nun until then?"

"If that's what it takes, yes." She turned back to Thumper, gave him a gentle hug. "You can tell your assistant I won't need that room at the Marriott. I'm staying here."

"In Thumper's stall?"

She nodded. "Or outside on the floor. I don't care."

She thought Ty might argue, but he must've realized the futility of arguing. "Can I get you something before I leave?"

"No," she said sharply.

"Then I'll see you tomorrow."

"You don't have to hold my hand through this," she said.

"You're right, Caroline. I don't. But I'll be here for you anyway because I'm a part of this…whether you like it or not. Remember, I have a vested interest in you and your horse."

She wanted to argue with him, but what could she say? She couldn't afford to lose Harrison's as a sponsor, not if she hoped to continue competing on a professional level.

She glanced back at Thumper.

If she ever competed again…

Chapter Eight

I couldn't focus this morning...because of you.

Ty walked away from Thumper's stall, diverse emotions swirling through him. Anger, disbelief, but most of all, an uneasiness that settled deep in the pit of his stomach. Was it really his fault her horse had been injured? He knew improperly warming up an animal could lead to injury. But had he really distracted her that much?

"Damn," he muttered under his breath.

He didn't know. Didn't care, actually. The important thing was to get Thumper well. He would deal with Caroline on a personal level later.

"Miss Sheppard would like to stay the night here with her horse," Ty said to the first person he came across, the same assistant who'd escorted them into the building earlier. "Is that possible?"

"Of course," she said. "I'll set it up."

And so he drove to the hotel alone, and as he checked in, all he felt was apprehension. No, he didn't own her, but he wanted to get to know her. Despite her objections.

And that was odd.

Normally, if a woman told him to stay away, he moved on.

Normally.

But things hadn't been normal since the moment he'd first seen Caroline's picture.

He let himself into his room, a plush two-bedroom suite that his father—a rancher at heart—would have scoffed at. "Slim" Harrison preferred things simple. No cherrywood furniture or plush beds. No spacious quarters at three hundred dollars a night. Give his father a sleeping bag on the ground and that's where he'd be most comfortable.

I couldn't focus…because of you.

My father always told me I could do it.

Ty stared out at the view that was considered one of the best in Baton Rouge. It was late afternoon. He wondered if Caroline had made arrangements for the care of her other horses. But of course she would. Mike would likely handle it.

A plane circled the sky, no doubt on its way to the busy airport. Patches of green broke up the monotony of a vista filled with skyscrapers and parking lots. Somewhere off to his left Caroline sat with her horse, probably thinking her chances to make the NFR were over.

My father always told me I could do it.

Ty plucked his cell phone from his pocket and dialed. His dad answered on the third ring.

"Have you been arrested?" Slim asked the moment he picked up.

"No."

"Are giraffes falling from the sky?"

"Dad."

"Well, I don't know why else you'd be calling me."

"We ran into a problem with the shoot today."

"What happened?" his father asked, and to Ty's surprise, he sounded concerned. Ever since Ty had taken over Harrison's Boots, he'd seen less and less of his father. But that was probably a good thing. He and his father had never really seen eye to eye.

"Miss Sheppard's horse broke a leg."

"Oh, that's too bad. Did she have to put the animal down?"

"No. Not yet at least. Hopefully not ever. They're operating tomorrow."

"Operating, huh? Like they did to that Kentucky Derby winner?"

"Something like that," Ty said.

"Well, let's hope this ends more happily for Miss Sheppard."

"Caro's pretty broken up."

"I imagine she would be," Slim said. "That's a tough situation."

"I wish there was something more I could do for her."

His dad was silent for a moment. "You like this woman, don't you?"

"What makes you say that?"

"I've seen her picture," Slim said.

"She's our spokesperson, Dad. Of course I'm concerned about her."

"That's not what I meant, and you know it."

Ty followed the progress of a car down on the street below, watching as it stopped at a red light. "What did you mean?"

"Your reputation precedes you, son."

"I don't believe this," Ty muttered, wondering why he'd called.

"I'm still in touch with people. People who know you. And they tell me it's a different woman every month."

The car below moved on, the light below having turned green. "I fail to see what this has to do with Caroline Sheppard. Our *spokesperson*."

"Aww, don't hand me that hog wash," Slim said. "She's just your type. Smart. Pretty. Athletic."

Ty bit back an oath. How did his father know? Had it gotten that bad? Had he dated so many women in recent years that his dad was able to deduce his "type" by simply glancing at a picture?

Apparently so.

"You shouldn't mix business with pleasure. You know what happens when you do that."

"Thanks for reminding me," Ty all but growled.

His father referred to the time Ty had dated a Harrison's employee—the *only* time. Two months later, when the affair had ended, Ty'd had to hire an attorney to fight a bogus sexual harassment suit. She'd sure gotten even for being dumped.

"Look, son. If you like her as a friend, that's fine. Buy her a horse or something. That ought to show her you care."

"Dad, I hardly think that would be appropriate."

"Why not?"

"Besides," Ty said, watching cars now fly through the intersection, "I don't know the first thing about barrel horses."

"Yeah, but I bet you could find someone who does."

Mike. Caro's friend. Ty shook his head. "Caro wouldn't accept any help from me."

"Why not? Your stalking of her aside, Harrison's is her sponsor."

"I'm not stalking her."

"You keep after her like you are, and she'll think so."

"What makes you think I'm pursuing her?" Ty asked, fed up with defending himself.

"Because you've been pursuing a lot of women since your mother died."

Ty straightened. "That's not true."

"Isn't it, son?"

Ty ran a hand through his hair. He'd examine that statement later. "My social life aside, she won't accept a new horse from me."

"Then *I'll* buy her one," Slim said.

"Same difference."

"We can *both* be her *friend*."

"Dad."

He heard his father chuckle. Ty realized that his father was pulling his leg and that was…unusual.

"Well, if *as a friend* you won't buy her a new horse, the least you can do is make sure the injured one has the best care."

"I've sent our jet out to pick up Caro's brother. He's a vet."

"Well, there you go," Slim said. "Sounds like you're being a *good* friend."

Ty shook his head. This conversation was going nowhere fast…as usual.

"In the meantime," his father continued, "have that fancy hotel of yours make you a warm glass of milk. Your mom used to swear that gave her pleasant dreams. If you're worried about your friend, maybe it'll help you sleep."

His mother.

Ty switched the phone to his other ear. "Dad, I've got to go."

"Well then. Let me know how it goes," Slim said.

"I will."

But when Slim heard his son break the connection he continued to stare at the phone. Something wasn't right. For the first time since his beloved Beth's passing, Ty sounded genuinely concerned about something other than Harrison's Boots. Was it really about a wounded horse? Or was it something more?

Who *was* this Caroline Sheppard?

Slim stared out his kitchen window, frowning. Maybe he'd take a trip down to Louisiana and find out. He'd given Ty plenty of space over the years, but maybe it was time to change all that.

Maybe it was time to show his son that he wasn't the only one feeling alone.

Chapter Nine

Caro tossed and turned the whole night. Every time Thumper moved, she shot up from her cot. Nine times out of ten it was nothing, but every once in a while the paint would cock his ears toward her, his expression clearly asking her what was wrong with him.

It broke Caro's heart.

"We'll get you all fixed up," she said, stroking him. "I promise."

"You must be Caroline Sheppard."

Caro looked up. She'd had visitors all morning. One after the other, LSU veterinary staff had stopped by to introduce themselves, and so she assumed the gray-haired man was yet another doctor. Except he didn't look the part. With his battered felt hat and work-worn shirt, he looked like a horse trainer, especially with his tan skin and wind-chapped lips.

"I am," she said softly, trying hard not to startle Thumper.

The man didn't say anything for a moment, just studied her. Then she heard him mutter, "Whew, you sure are a pretty little thing. Your pictures don't do you justice."

She wrinkled her brow, glanced back at Thumper for a moment and then walked toward the new arrival. "I'm sorry, you are...?"

"Slim Harrison," he said. "And this must be Thumper, although I'm sorry to say he's not looking too good."

Slim Harrison? This man was Ty's *father?*

But of course he was. Caro could see a slight resemblance now. They had the same green eyes and square jaw. Even the same slight smile. But whereas the younger Harrison was all spit and polish, Ty's father had the well-worn look of an old saddle. Tall and slightly stooped, he walked with a hitch when she motioned for him to come in.

"Poor old boy," he said, patting the paint's neck. "They got you hitched up like a piece of four-legged cargo, don't they?"

"It's keeping his weight off his legs."

"Oh, I'm sure," Slim said. "But I can't imagine it feels good to have a strap around your belly."

"It was a long night," she said. "For both of us."

And today would be an even longer day. Her brother was due to arrive at any moment, Dr. Danson in tow. The surgery was set for ten o'clock, and Caro hoped the time would fly by. Then again, perhaps she should hope for it to go slow. These might be her last few hours with...

No. She wouldn't think that way.

"You look worn-out, too," Ty's father said.

Caro gazed into his kind eyes. They really were remarkably like Ty's. "I didn't get much sleep," she admitted.

"I can understand why." Slim moved his hand down Thumper's neck. "One of my cutting horses fractured a coffin bone once. Freak accident while coming out of a trailer. Took one step, then just about fell to the ground. We thought we might lose him, too, but he recovered. Our vet says that bone's stronger now than it was before. What's more, the horse went on to win the national championship a few years back."

"You raise cutting horses?" Caro asked, shocked.

"Ty didn't tell you?" Slim asked, his hand resting on Thumper's neck.

"No. All he said was that you were the cattle rancher in the family."

"We raise some of the finest cutting horses in the nation. So don't let Ty's spit and polish fool you. There isn't a bigger cowboy at heart than my son, but he does his duty by us with our company. I tip my hat to him, too, 'cause I never wanted a thing to do with it."

Thumper pricked his ears, his nostrils flaring as if he smelled something or someone. Caro looked up, but there wasn't anyone outside the stall.

"Ty's an upstanding man," Slim said. "He may

come across as all-business, but deep down inside he's got a caring heart."

Yes, Caro thought. She'd caught a glimpse of that when they'd been talking by the trailers.

"He's kind of like your horse here. Looks like an ordinary old paint, albeit a bit beat-up at the moment. You wouldn't know by looking at him that inside beats the heart of a champion."

No, you wouldn't, Caro thought, her throat thickening. Ty's father *understood.* She loved Thumper not because he was an awesome barrel horse, but because he'd always been there for her. Good run or bad, off day or not, when it came time to load Thumper up after a race, she always knew he'd given his all.

"He kept trying to run for me," she murmured.

Slim nodded.

"I tried to pull him up, could tell something was wrong, but he just wanted to run."

"The heart of a champion," Slim repeated, moving to Thumper's head. "I can see it in his eyes. That's what you've got to do. Look at the depth of someone's soul."

"Whose soul—"

"Dad!"

Ty's cry caused her to turn. And there he was, the man as responsible as Thumper for her sleepless night.

"What are you doing here?" he asked in surprise.

Slim tipped his hat back and patted Thumper. "Figured I'd come and see what all the fuss was about. But I think I came for nothing. This guy's going to be all right, I can tell, although I can't say I truly wasted a trip. It's been a pleasure to meet his owner."

Caro thought Ty and his father couldn't be more different…and yet alike. She could see that now. They were both tanned and fit. By studying Slim, Caro knew she could catch a glimpse of what Ty would look like thirty years from now.

"When did you get here?" Ty asked.

"This morning." His dad stroked Thumper's cheek. "Hitched a ride with one of my quarter horse buddies. They were headed down this way for a show."

"I can't believe—"

"Where is she?"

Caro stiffened. That had sounded like Rand.

"Hey, little sis."

"Rand!"

"Aww," he said, his smile fading into a grimace. "Poor Thumper."

Thumper's head bobbed as if agreeing with Rand. She felt her eyes begin to burn yet again. Thumper stared at her brother as if he recognized the tall, dark-haired man, too.

"Come here," Rand said to Caro. "You look like you could use a hug."

"I can," she said, feeling tears begin to well.

"Oh, no," someone else said. "I don't think so. I'm first in line for a hug."

Rand stepped aside. "Mom?" Caro asked, her mouth suddenly slack.

"Come here, baby," her mother said gently. "Let me give you a hug."

Caro felt herself falter the moment she sank into her mother's arms. For the first time since Thumper had been injured, she knew she was about to lose it—really, truly lose it. And in front of Ty Harrison and his father.

"Mom," she said, squeezing her eyes shut, as if that might stop the flow of tears.

"Poor baby," Martha Sheppard said. "I know this has got to be tough for you."

"Thumper's hurt." Caro stated the obvious, her voice nearly a wail.

"I know, honey. That's why we're all here. Dr. Danson is out front talking to your vet. We're going to get Thumper all fixed up."

"I wanted to ride him in the NFR," Caro said, inhaling to keep her emotions at bay.

She would not bawl her eyes out. She would not.

"Who cares about the NFR? You could have been killed. But you're *okay*. That's all that matters," Martha said.

"*Thumper* matters."

"I know, honey. I know. But we'll fix him up. Rand and his friend will see to that."

Caro sniffed, wiped her eyes. Her throat was still thick with the effort to hold back tears. "How's it look?" she asked her brother, who was standing outside the stall, peering at the radiographs pinned to a light screen.

"It's broken, all right," he said. "But I've seen worse."

"You have?"

"Yup. Back when I was in school. We had a race horse come in with a fracture of the first phalanx," Rand said, pulling his wide shoulders back as he straightened. "It was in pieces, but we pinned it all together and the horse ended up being good as new a year later."

Caro felt hope buoy her spirits for the first time. But it was more than simply hearing Rand's positive outlook, it was that she now had with her not one, but *two* loved ones to help see her through the coming, emotion-filled hours. And one of them was her mom.

Her mom.

Caro felt tears burn the corners of her eyes again. Darn it. Since when had she become such a crybaby?

"Did you get any sleep last night?" the older woman asked, tilting her head as she studied her.

"No," Caro said. "Not really."

"Ty told us you refused to stay in a hotel," Martha said, holding her hand up against her cheek. Caro almost closed her eyes. "You can't do that, Caroline. You need to take care of yourself."

"But, Mom—"

"No but Mom-ing me," she said, stepping back.

"Tonight you go to the hotel, the sooner the better. Once we get Thumper patched up, I'm going to drive you there myself."

"But, Mom, what about Thumper? Who will watch him?"

Martha grasped her shoulders with both hands. "Caroline Winifred Sheppard, don't worry about your horse. He's got the best vets around, including your brother."

Caro sniffed, took a deep breath, pulled herself together. "I'm just afraid we won't be able to fix him up."

"There's no need to think that. Not with Rand here," Martha said, glancing to her right.

Caro followed her gaze. Slim Harrison stood there. "That's Ty's father, Slim."

"How do you do, Mr. Harrison," Martha said, holding out her hand. "I'm Martha Sheppard."

"Nice to meet you, ma'am," he said.

She turned back to Caroline. "Come on," she said. "Let's get some food in you."

"I'd rather stay here."

"When was the last time you had food in your belly?" Martha asked.

Caro didn't say anything.

"Uh-huh." She nodded. "That's what I thought."

"There's a cafeteria at the main school, if you want to walk that far," suggested Dr. Franklin, head of large-animal orthopedics. "It's a nice day outside and we've got some work to do here. You'd be doing us a favor to stay out of the way. Once we're ready to take him in, we'll call your cell phone."

"There you go," Martha said. "Let's stay out of their way. A walk will put some color in your cheeks, anyway."

"Hi," said another man, a little older than Rand. "I'm Dr. Danson."

"Thanks for coming," Caro said.

"Glad to help out," he said with a kindly smile. He was short, but he had the long, slender fingers of a surgeon.

"Come on," her mom said. "Let's go."

"I'll come with you," Ty said, his first words in a while. "If that's okay."

Caro thought about it for a moment. Last night she'd been silly to blame him for what had happened to Thumper, and she knew better now. Deep down inside she'd accepted the fact that she had nobody to blame but herself. Once again she'd let a man get in her head.

"Sure."

She saw Ty's shoulders relax, saw his slight smile. She had to look away because she didn't like the way that smile made her feel.

"I'll come, too," Slim said. "Get out of the way of all these doctors."

Why not? Caro thought, thinking there was no way on earth she'd be able to eat. No way.

Chapter Ten

She was right.

Food tasted like wood chips. Her palms were sweaty when she picked up her fork, and she couldn't help but wonder why she'd ever agreed to leave Thumper's side.

They don't need you, Caro.

She knew they didn't. There was to be more nuclear imaging this morning. After that all vets on staff would confer and then they'd go in and... operate.

She nearly choked on a bite of egg.

"You okay?" Ty said.

Slim and her mom were conversing across the table. The two of them certainly seemed to have hit it off. They really didn't have a whole lot to smile about, but Caro had seen her mom's grin once or twice.

"I'm all right," she said, setting her fork down. "Just nervous."

"You have a right to be."

She nodded, gazing out over the campus. They'd brought their food outside, and LSU had to be one of the prettiest colleges in the country. The tall, stately buildings were interspersed with trees where long, sprawling limbs sheltered students from the sun. Not that it was terribly hot this time of year.

"Caro, I hate to bring this up, but Bill, the director, called this morning. He's definitely going to need some voice work done for the commercial. I realize now is not the time to schedule something, but just so you know."

She shrugged, because really, what difference did it make? Her season was over. She might as well do something constructive while checking in on Thumper. "Just tell me where and when."

"Thanks."

"No. Thank *you*," she said softly. "For everything. You've been great and I'm…" she swallowed, her throat dry "…I'm really sorry for what I said last night. I know what happened to Thumper isn't your fault."

She thought he might say something, but he held her gaze for a long moment first. "You don't have to apologize," he murmured. "I know that was just the stress talking."

"It was, but it's better now, thanks to your flying in my mom. That was your doing, wasn't it?"

He nodded, his eyes nearly the same color as the

grass that dotted the campus. "I called her last night and asked if she wanted to tag along. Needless to say, she didn't have to think about it long."

"No. I suppose not," Caro said with a small smile.

Her cell phone rang.

Caro's heart just about stopped. She recognized the area code of the caller.

"This is it," she told her mom, Slim and Tyler.

"Caroline Sheppard?" a woman asked when she picked up. "We'll be taking Thumper into surgery in less than an hour."

"Okay, thank you," she said, snapping her phone closed. "Let's go."

They were the longest, most nerve-racking hours of Caro's life. She'd wanted to be in the surgical room with Thumper, but the LSU staff had vetoed that idea. She was forced to wait in a room near the front of the main building. Caro paced from one end of the waiting room to the other, all the while stealing glances at the clock.

"We're done."

It was Rand. Caro had always been a little awed by the sight of her brother in blue scrubs. He had a white mask pulled down around his neck and a surgical cap on his head, and there was a slight smile on his lips.

"It went well?" Caro asked, her voice rising.

"It went well. The break was a simple one, Caro,

just as all the tests revealed. We put two screws in, one on the back and one on the front. In a couple weeks' time Thumper should be putting weight on that leg again. In a few weeks, he'll be walking almost normally."

"Oh, thank God," Martha said.

Caro squeezed her eyes shut, turning away so no one had to watch her cry.

"Caro," Ty said. "It's all right," he murmured, enfolding her in his arms. She rested his head against his chest and let go. Funny, too, because just that morning she hadn't wanted to cry in front of him and his dad, and yet here she was, bawling her eyes out in his arms.

"Shh."

"It's okay, honey," she heard her mom say. "Let it all out."

Rand came up to her, too; she could tell when his big hand clapped her on the shoulder. She realized then just how stressed she'd been over the whole thing, how afraid she'd been that Thumper would go down…and never wake up again.

"Thank you," she said, drawing back and looking at her brother—at them all. "Thank you guys so much for being here for me."

"Aw, honey," her mom said, hugging her next. "Where else would I be but with my little girl?"

Thanks to Ty, Caro reminded herself. Ty and his private jet. He'd taken the extra step—gone above and beyond—to take care of her and her horse.

She looked into Ty's eyes. "Thank you."

Something passed between them, a current of something that felt almost like electricity but settled with a warm glow in her heart.

"You're welcome," Ty said.

Caro wiped her eyes. "Can I go see him?"

"Not yet," Rand said. "He's in isolation right now. It'll be a few hours."

"Then you should go get some sleep," her mother said, ever the caregiver.

"Mom. I can't sleep right now."

"You want to bet?" she said. "Let Rand stay here with Thumper. If anything happens, I'm sure he'll give you a call."

"I'd still rather stay."

"No," her mom said firmly. "Stubborn girl. You go with Ty back to the hotel, which you should have stayed at last night. Slim here can take me to our hotel."

"You're not staying at the Marriott?"

"I had my assistant book a hotel that was closer, so Rand could be nearby," Ty interjected.

Of course he had, Caro thought. He was good at thinking ahead.

"Go," Martha said.

"Go," Rand echoed. "I'll call you if anything changes."

And so she went.

She fell asleep before they reached the I-10.

He'd rented a large SUV, one with plush seats that

Caro sank into, her head dropping to the side practically the moment he turned on the ignition. He let her sleep, admiring the long, blond hair that spilled over her shoulder. He'd never, not in all his years, wanted to stare at a woman like he wanted to sit and stare at Caroline Sheppard. But he had to drive.

She didn't stir when he neared their hotel, and so instead of turning into the valet parking, he turned left, toward the Mississippi River. There were parks all along the riverbank, brown signs pointing the way. He found an isolated spot overlooking the river, which moved so slowly it almost appeared to be still.

What would he do about Caroline?

His gut told him to woo her. But to be honest, Ty had never wooed a woman in his life. What was it about this one that made her so special?

Tyler parked the SUV in the shade of a cypress tree and turned toward Caro. She looked even more beautiful asleep. He didn't know how that could be, because he'd always thought her best feature was her gray eyes. But even with her lids closed, she took his breath away. Her lips were soft and full, and he was tempted to lean across the seat and kiss her. But he didn't. Fortunate, because just then his cell phone rang. She stirred as he checked the number. His office. They could wait, he thought, shutting the front cover.

"We're not at the hotel."

He put his phone back on the dash. "No. I thought I'd let you sleep."

She must have fallen asleep hard, because she blinked a few times before getting her bearings. "Is that the Mississippi?"

"It is."

"Pretty," she murmured, her eyes large and sleepy.

"Yes." He didn't mean the river.

Ty felt his breathing change as they looked at each other.

"Caro," he said, clutching the steering wheel to keep from pulling her to him. Or better yet, guiding her to the bench seat behind them, where he could lay her down and cover her with kisses.

"What?"

His knuckles turned white. He had to think fast to come up with something impersonal to say. "I want to encourage you to keep riding and trying for the NFR."

She didn't say anything, but looked away.

"I know it's probably the last thing you want to think about right now, but I wanted to encourage you to do it."

Why?

Why did he want to kiss her so badly? What *was* this that he felt toward her? He felt almost…besotted. That was a good word, if a bit old-fashioned. He glanced over at her, captivated by her lips.

"It would be a waste of time."

It took effort to release the steering wheel.

"I have a feeling you're wrong," he said quietly, steeling himself before turning toward her. "About a lot of things."

"What do you mean?" she asked, something in her own eyes alerting him to the fact that she felt it, too. The same, unmistakable current of attraction that made his blood stir and his body tingle.

"I want you, Caro. Now more than ever. I know you told me to keep my distance, but I can't and, to be honest, I'm tired of fighting it."

"Ty, don't—"

He unbuckled his seat belt, his hands suddenly shaking. "Let me kiss you once, Caro, and if there's nothing there, I'll leave you alone."

"That's not a good idea."

"Why not?" he asked. "You feel it, don't you? Every time we're near each other it's like dancing with an open wire."

"I can't, Ty. Not now. Maybe in a few months—"

"No," he said. "Now." And at last he touched her.

She shivered, but didn't pull away. Ty felt triumphant. She didn't resist, just closed her eyes as his fingers caressed her jaw, his thumb brushing the sensitive spot beneath her ear.

"Caroline."

She closed her eyes, murmured. "Please, call me Caro. I always feel like I'm in trouble—"

He kissed her.

Chapter Eleven

Caro arched into him immediately, because it was true, she *did* feel it. What's more, she *wanted* to feel it.

His kiss changed, turned into something impossible to resist, an openmouthed, hungry possession that made her moan in the back of her throat. He tasted like vanilla coffee. The fingers he'd used to brush her cheek dropped to her neck, stroking the back of it so that she shivered with pleasure. Delicious warmth spread down her spine, along her sides and then to her center.

It had been so long since she'd experienced pleasure.

"Ty," she murmured, her hand curling around his nape. His hair was soft there, and curly, as it slid through her fingers. "We shouldn't."

"We won't," he said, his breath warm against the side of her face as he turned his head away, holding her against him, pressing her cheek against his own. "Not if you don't want to."

She *shouldn't* want to. She hardly knew him, and yet she was paralyzed by longing.

"I think, maybe, I'm going to regret this."

His body went still. She felt the tension beneath her hands, but then it faded, replaced by another kind of tautness.

He kissed her again.

But this time it was no gentle, tentative meeting of the lips. This time it was a full-on assault—as if he'd been holding back, afraid to let her feel just how much he wanted her.

She kissed him back just as passionately.

His hand moved down her neck, toward her collarbone. She could feel her breasts heat and then tighten in anticipation of his touch.

Yes, it had been far too long.

But he didn't touch her there, not right away. His hand slipped beneath the button-down shirt she wore. He fingered her bare skin and she felt goose bumps.

"Yes," she whispered. It was as good as she'd intuitively known it would be. His touch was masterful, his fingers sure and strong as they slowly, inexorably slid toward her bra. He found her nipple, pulled the edge of her cup down, whirled his thumb around the sensitive tip, teasing it and making her want far more than just his hand on her breast.

She reached down between them. Somehow she found herself sideways on the seat, her back against the door.

She cupped him.

It was his turn to gasp. And there could be no mistaking where this would lead. He was hard for her, but she made him harder, her fingers sliding up the length of him, the denim warm beneath her touch.

"Caro," he grunted, pulling her toward him, guiding her to the backseat.

She let him, arching toward him when he found the snap of her jeans. She didn't care that they were in a park, out in the middle of nowhere. Or that someone walking by might be able to see them. She wanted him. *Now.*

He pulled at her pants, and then she was naked from the waist down, and he was bending and spreading her legs….

Oh, Lord. He wasn't—

She leaned her head back, her elbows resting on the leather seat. She shouldn't let him. It was too intimate. They didn't know each other well enough.

But she was beyond being inhibited.

The first touch of his tongue made her groan. The second caused her to pant. By the third she was lost to the silky sensation of him caressing her flesh, teasing it, suckling it.

She moaned again, half in protest at such wanton behavior. But then his tongue found her center and she was lost.

"Oh, Ty."

One last caress and she was over the edge; it

happened that fast. Her body seized and then expanded as pleasure radiated through every limb, every bone. "Ty!"

Nothing would ever be the same again.

"Get dressed."

Caro's eyes snapped open.

"What?"

"I'm not making love to you in the back of a rental car."

"Well, no, but I—"

He tossed her pants at her. He had to get her covered up, because the sight of her lying there, her legs spread wide...

God help him.

It took everything he had not to jump on her like a teenager, turn the windows foggy with their passion....

Stoically he climbed back into the driver's seat, relaxing only fractionally when he heard her begin to slide her pants back on.

"Ty, I'm not so certain that was smart."

He jerked around to face her. "What?"

The SUV still might smell of her sweetly released passion, but she suddenly looked uncomfortable. "You're my sponsor. We're supposed to have a professional relationship. I can't—"

"Don't," he interrupted. "Don't even go there. I'm not a patient man when it comes to things I want."

She settled warily in the seat next to him. "You're upset."

"Of course," he said. "Caro, I'm tired of being patient. I've felt this thing simmering between us but I kept my distance, mostly because that's what you seemed to want."

"So that night by the trailer you really did want to kiss me?"

"Yes. I did," he admitted. "I wasn't honest with you that night. But I didn't want to frighten you, or for you to know I was fighting this attraction."

"So you lied."

He released a frustrated breath. "No. Not really. I don't think even *I* knew what I wanted then. But I've never held back when I've wanted something— personally or professionally."

She stared over at him. Outside the SUV the river continued to glide by, but inside the cab Ty felt as if he were drowning.

"I feel something for you, Caro. At first I thought it might be because you're the most beautiful woman I've ever met—"

"Ty—"

"No. Let me finish. But that's not it. You are beautiful," he said, reaching for her hand. "But there's so much more to you than that."

She didn't say anything, just continued to stare at him.

"I feel the strangest urge to woo you, Caro. Court

you, if you will. And that's what I intend to do…if you'll let me."

She looked as if she didn't know what to say. He squeezed her hand.

"Let me take you back to the hotel," he said. "Let me make love to you properly, not in the backseat of an SUV."

"I don't know," she murmured, her gaze dropping to their clasped hands. "This is all so sudden."

"But it's right. Surely you can feel that."

She looked up, stared into his eyes unflinchingly. "I do feel it, Ty," she all but whispered. "I do. But everything's such a mess right now. My career is in such a shambles—"

"No, it's not. We're still going to sponsor you. Whatever horse you want to ride, we'll be there."

"I know," she said. "I never had any doubts about that."

"Then what?"

He watched her take a deep breath, felt her fingers clench around his. "I need to think about it," she said. "I know that's not fair." She squeezed harder. "That you must want to pick me up and throw me down on that backseat."

"You have no idea."

"I do," she said. "I really, really do. But I'm afraid to go beyond what we just did."

"What we just did is nothing compared to how it will be when I make love to you."

PLAY THE
Lucky Key Game

Do You Have the LUCKY KEY?

and you can get

FREE BOOKS
and **FREE GIFTS!**

Scratch the gold areas with a coin. Then check below to see the books and gifts you can get!

YES!
I have scratched off the gold areas. Please send me the 2 FREE BOOKS and 2 FREE GIFTS for which I qualify. I understand I am under no obligation to purchase any books, as explained on the back of this card.

(H-AR-06/07)

354 HDL EL4S   154 HDL ELUH

FIRST NAME	LAST NAME

ADDRESS

APT.#	CITY

STATE / PROV.	ZIP/POSTAL CODE

www.eHarlequin.com

🔑🔑🔑🔑 2 free books plus 2 free gifts   🔑🔑🔑🔑 1 free book

🔑🔑🔑🔑 2 free books   🔑🔑🔑🔑 Try Again!

She swallowed. "I know. And I think that's what frightens me." She leaned forward, kissed his cheek, murmuring, "Slow down, cowboy."

Slow down.

He let go of her hand, sat back in his seat. Damn it. He didn't want to wait.

But he would.

For her.

For her, he suddenly realized, he would do just about anything.

"I think it would be best if I dropped you off at the hotel."

She wore an expression that was sympathetic, yet also relieved. "No problem."

"But first I think I'm going to take a swim in the Mississippi."

She laughed, not loudly, just a soft rumble that sounded like a kitten's purr. He had to grab the steering wheel once more.

"I don't think I'd blame you."

Chapter Twelve

They let her see Thumper later that evening, but only for a short time, and only, she suspected, because Rand pulled some strings. Ty drove her over, Caro stealing glances at him the whole way. Not once did he mention what had happened earlier in the park. In fact, he acted like a perfect gentleman, opening her door for her when they arrived.

"Thank you," she said as she slipped out.

He didn't need to be told what she was thanking him for. She could tell by the way his jaw tightened that it had been tough for him to drive away from the hotel.

"You're welcome," he said.

They wouldn't let Ty go with her, so she made her way to the large-animal recovery area on her own.

Thumper looked like hell.

Of course, she hadn't expected him to be in peak condition, but she'd been hoping to find some kind of spark, a glint in her horse's eyes. He just appeared miserable.

"Poor guy," she said over and over again. But as she stared, reality set in fast. He was wounded. Would be lucky to compete again. She'd lost her best horse and she honestly didn't know where that left her. It'd take a miracle to make it to the NFR, and after Thumper's successful operation she was fresh out of those.

"You don't look happy."

Rand.

Her brother stood outside the stall.

She put a hand under her horse's neck and pressed her face against his mane. "I was just thinking," she said simply.

"About the NFR."

She never could keep stuff from him.

"There's always next year, Caro," Rand said.

She stepped back, the smell of her horse still in her nose. Thumper looked so awful that she immediately felt bad for whining about the competition.

"You're right. All I want is for him to recover."

Rand followed her gaze. "But you're still thinking about the NFR."

"I'm such a selfish brat."

"No, you're not," he said with a slight chuckle. "You're human. You've suffered a huge setback. It's only natural that you should think about what you've lost."

"I still feel bad for doing it."

"He'll get better."

"I know."

"And in the meantime, don't forget, you've got Classy to ride," he answered. "Last time you were at the ranch she ran pretty well. Maybe you should give her a shot."

"And maybe I should just forget about it all. Find a place nearby and stay with Thumper."

"Can you afford to do that?"

She couldn't even afford the coming vet bill.

"I was talking to your boyfriend earlier," Rand said.

They'd warned her that she needed to keep her visit short, and so with one last pat, she left the stall, looking up at her brother the moment she shut the door. "He's *not* my boyfriend."

"That's not the impression I got. But anyway, we were talking on the way out here from the airport. Ty was saying he'd pay to keep Thumper here as long as it took him to recover. That's a great offer, Caro. You and I both know how expensive your bill's going to be. My friend will give you a break, but I doubt the other vets will. With Thumper in such excellent care, you'd be free to get back on the rodeo trail. You might even still make the NFR."

She almost argued that point, but she was getting sick of trying to explain to everyone that she just didn't have a shot anymore. "Right now I can't even think about that."

"But you need to," Rand said, his expression utterly serious. "You can't just throw in the towel, Caro. You have two perfectly good horses you can ride as backup. Heck, that's why you always bring those darn horses along—in the event that something happens. Well, it has, and you have nothing to stop you from climbing back in the saddle."

"My heart wouldn't be in it."

"So that's what you're going to do? Walk away?"

"As you said, there's always next year."

He frowned, shook his head. If he'd been wearing his cowboy hat he probably would have taken it off and shoved a hand through his hair. "You're giving up, aren't you, Caro?"

Her heart started to pound. "Rand…"

"You are, aren't you?"

"No."

Her brother's eyes narrowed. He glanced back at Thumper, then to her, the fluorescent lights illuminating his disappointed expression. "Once before, I watched you walk away. I'll be damned if I'll let you do it again. Not without a fight."

She winced, almost told him that was a low blow. But did her brother have a point? Was she quitting because of Thumper's injury or because she was interested in Ty?

"Before you say no, just think about it," Rand said. "And think about what Dad would have said, too."

Rand was right. If their dad were still alive, he'd be asking her the same questions. "Okay, I'll think about it."

"You look upset," Ty said, standing up when he saw her enter the waiting room.

"I'm just tired," she said, glancing around the space, which looked like any other veterinarian clinic waiting room the world over, with its linoleum floor, plastic chairs and fake plants. "Have you seen my mom?"

He scratched the back of his neck, his expression somewhat bemused. "She and Dad came by, and when they heard no visitors were allowed, they decided to go to dinner. Your mom said she'd call you later."

Caro raised her eyebrows. "Dinner, huh?"

"Yup," Ty said with a nod. "And I was hoping we could do the same thing."

Once before, I watched you walk away, her brother had said.

She turned toward the glass partition, where a few assistants were talking. Funny, she hadn't even noticed them there earlier when she'd been waiting for word on Thumper. "I need to get a copy of my bill."

"Already paid."

She turned back to him.

"I'm your sponsor, remember?"

"I can pay you back," she said.

With what, Caro? Thumper's good looks? While she was certain her mom would offer to pay, Caro wouldn't let her do it.

"There's no need to do that," he murmured, stepping toward her. When he got close enough, he cupped her jaw with one hand. "I'd do it even if I wasn't your sponsor."

Things had changed so rapidly between them. She could barely keep up.

"Ty, I—"

"There you are, Caro," Rand said, coming through the door into the waiting area. He stopped short when he saw Ty standing there, his palm pressed to her cheek.

"Uh, Rand. Hi. I thought you were staying with Thumper." Her cheeks flushed, especially when her brother's gaze flitted between the two of them.

"No need," he said.

Ty's hand fell to his side.

"There's enough vets on call I don't have to stick around. I was thinking I might go to dinner." Rand nudged her shoulder in a challenge. "Want to come along?"

Caro looked at Ty.

"*We* were going to dinner," Ty said. "But you're welcome to join us."

Rand all but smirked. "No thanks," he said. "I'll find something on my own."

"You need a ride?" Caro asked.

"Nope. I've already called a cab."

"We can drop you off," Ty offered.

"That's okay," Rand said. "I'll see you guys later."
He sauntered outside.

Caro's heart began to thump like a galloping
horse.

Once before, I watched you walk away....

She wasn't going to walk away this time, damn
it. She wanted to compete.

Competing meant no Ty. Already he'd proved
what a distraction he could be. Never again.

"I have to go," she said.

"Go?" Ty asked. "Where? To dinner?"

"No, Ty," she said quietly. "Back to the rodeo
grounds, to my horses."

"I thought Mike was taking care of them."

"Mike can't drive them to Dallas."

"Dallas?"

"That's where I'm entered next."

He looked as if he didn't know what to say. "You
mean you want to go visit your horses?"

"No, Ty," she said. "I want to take them to Dallas
so I can compete with them there."

"But, I thought…" His whole body seemed to
slump. "You're going for the NFR on Classy."

"Yes."

"Which means no 'us.'"

She almost told him there'd never been an "us."

"I have to, Ty. Even you said so yourself. And you're right, that means no men in my life. You're already in my head enough. That's bad."

"Bad? Why?"

The vet assistants on the other side of the glass obviously couldn't hear them, but still, she lowered her voice. "I can't ride and date at the same time."

"Why not?"

"Because it never works out."

"I'm not that first guy, Caro. The one who broke your heart."

"I know you're not David," she said. "You're an even bigger problem."

"What do you mean?"

In the background, a phone rang. Someone answered it right away. "David pursued me for months, Ty. You've slipped under my defenses in a matter of days."

He gently clasped her by the forearms. "That's not bad, Caro. That's a good thing."

"Not for me."

"Why not?" he asked, and she could tell he was getting frustrated.

"Because look what happened the last time I was distracted by you."

She didn't need to say anything more. She saw the guilt in his eyes. Their very surroundings seemed to emphasize her point.

"I'd stay out of your way."

"Yeah, but for how long? One of these days you'd get tired of standing in the background."

"We won't know that unless we try."

"I'm not going to try."

"So that's it. It's over before it really started?"

She nodded. "It has to be. And if you don't understand why, then you don't understand *me*."

He shook his head in disbelief. "Let me take you to dinner. We can talk this out—"

"No. What I need is for you to take me to the rodeo grounds."

"Caro—"

"Now, Ty." Before he broke down her defenses. "Fine."

She tried not to let him see how much his attitude hurt her. She tried, too, to understand his point of view. He liked her but now she was dumping him. She knew only too well how that felt. Except *this* time, she wasn't on the receiving end. That was exactly how it should be.

Wasn't it?

Chapter Thirteen

He didn't say a word to her the whole way. Caro didn't really expect him to. If anything, his silence only reinforced her decision to end it. Obviously he wasn't the type of man who took feminine direction well.

Would you if the situation were reversed?

It didn't matter what she thought, she told herself firmly. It didn't matter what anyone thought. She needed to do whatever it took to win, and that included dumping Ty.

He dropped her off near the portable stalls. The rodeo was still in progress, and it seemed strange to Caro to be back where it had all started, with cowboys and cowgirls walking around as if nothing had happened. In their world nothing had, she realized. Just another day chasing a dream.

"Thanks for the ride," she said, staring out the SUV's front window, at the setting sun turning the sky a fiery red.

"You're welcome."

That was all he said. He didn't even look at her. Caro slipped out of the vehicle, then watched him drive away, her eyes burning.

Stupid, idiotic woman. You barely knew the man.

But she'd gotten to know him well enough.

"You're back!" Mike cried in delight.

Caro jumped, startled. She'd been walking blindly and hadn't even realized she was at her rig. "Hey, Mike."

"How's Thumper?" the big cowboy asked, giving her one of his patented smothering hugs.

"As well as can be expected, given what's wrong."

Mike's smile faded. "We were all sorry to hear about that, Caro. Everyone's hoping he'll make it back."

"I hope so, too," she said. "And in the meantime, I'm going to keep going on one of my backup horses."

"Atta girl."

"How are they?"

"Doing just fine," Mike said. "Eating their fool heads off in their stalls. You might want to take them out before you hit the road."

She'd do that.

"By the way," Mike said. "I thought you should know you're not out of the running yet."

"What?"

"Everyone's had a bad weekend. You're still in the money."

"No way."

"I'm serious," Mike said.

Caro was stunned, and for the first time since Thumper's injury, she felt hopeful. "Wow."

"So go get 'em, tiger."

She tried to do exactly that, all but throwing herself into getting ready for Dallas. She focused on her riding, or tried to….

Ty never called.

But if the situation were reversed, she wouldn't call, either. To be honest, she half expected him to pull his sponsorship. He didn't, and in some ways that made it worse. He truly was a decent man.

So she rode. Classy was a reliable mare, and one day she'd more than likely be great, but she was a lot of rodeos away from winning the finals. Still, Caro's hopes rose even more when she had a good run in Dallas. She didn't win, but she placed in the money. Suddenly, she really did still have a shot at making the NFR. And then one of the LSU vets called to tell her Thumper's latest X-rays looked promising. With any luck he'd be back in California by year's end. Good news indeed. She'd have gone out and celebrated if Annie, Ty's assistant, hadn't called.

"Hi, Annie," Caro said, her heart rate slowly returning to normal once she realized it wasn't Ty on the other end.

"Hello, Ms. Sheppard," the woman said, her voice perhaps too friendly. What could she want?

Caro didn't have long to wait for an answer.

"Actually," Annie said, "I'm calling to check your

availability this week. We need you to fly to our headquarters here in Cheyenne so we can finish up the voice-over work for your commercial. We've also decided to kill two birds with one stone by doing a photo shoot."

"What?" Caro asked. Mike was walking by and raised any eyebrow.

"Record the voice-overs for your commercial and do a—"

"No, no. I heard you," Caro said. "I'm just surprised. It's the end of the rodeo season, so I don't have time to go anywhere. Mr. Harrison knows that."

"He's aware of your scheduling conflicts, Miss Sheppard. That's why we'll be flying you to us."

She was about to tell the woman that it was more than a scheduling conflict, but figured she'd be wasting her breath. "May I speak to Mr. Harrison, please?" Caro said through gritted teeth.

"He's in a meeting right now."

"Tell him I'm on the line."

"Miss Sheppard, really, I can't interrupt—"

"Annie?" Caro cut her off. "I'm about to load up my horses. Once I'm under way, who knows if Mr. Harrison will be able to reach me at all. Cell phone service isn't exactly the best on Texas back roads. Please, if there's any chance that you can slip him a note, I'd appreciate it."

After a long silence, she heard a resigned sigh. "Hold, please."

Music came on. Caro tried to calm down. Ty wasn't doing this on purpose, she told herself. He wasn't trying to manipulate her. There had to be a reason why he was insisting she fly off to Cheyenne.

"Caroline?" It was his deep baritone.

And her heart tumbled over. It was so good to hear his voice.

"Hi, Ty."

No, no, no. You're not allowed to miss him.

"Annie tells me there's a problem."

"Ty," she said, "I can't fly to Cheyenne. That's crazy. I won't get to New Mexico for at least a day. And then I have to work Classy because, Lord knows, she needs all the miles she can get—"

"We'll fly you in after you ride in the morning," Ty said, sounding stern. "Pick the day."

She clenched her hand around the cell phone. "You do realize that this is a very important weekend."

"I do," he stated. "We'll have you back in time to ride the next morning."

And so what could she say? It was like the first time she'd met him, when he'd left her no choice but to agree. She hated when he did that.

He's only doing his job, Caro.

But she preferred not to think of her life that way—as part of his job. "Fine," she said. "I'll be in New Mexico by Tuesday. I can fly out Wednesday morning."

"I'll have Annie make the arrangements."

That's all he said. No "So how have you been?" No "Thank you." No "How's Thumper?" Just Annie's voice a few seconds later.

"Miss Sheppard," she said, "what town is your rodeo in?"

Ty rubbed his hands over his face, turning from the phone and staring out his office window. His chair skidded across the plastic mat. He watched as, down below, cars and buses traveled along Central Avenue, the sparkling vehicles at odds with the flat facades of the historic buildings that dotted the roadside. It always looked to him as if there should be cowboys and cattle milling below, and normally he enjoyed staring out the window of his 1890s office building.

Not today.

He'd known Caro wouldn't be happy about the photo shoot and voice-overs, but they'd bent over backward to accommodate her schedule. It was time she came to them.

Because he wanted to see her again.

Damn it.

"Mr. Harrison," Annie called, "they're still waiting for you in the conference room."

"I'm on my way," he told her, getting up from his chair and putting Caro out of his mind.

But instead of handing Caro over to one of his staff, three days later Ty found himself outside a hangar at the Cheyenne Regional Airport. The hangar housed Harrison Air—a rather grandiose name that made it seem as if they maintained a fleet of planes rather than the single Gulfstream jet. He got out of the backseat of the limo, the cool Wyoming air made chillier by the building's shadow. The driver tipped his hat. Ty hardly noticed. He heard a jet take off at the main airport behind the private terminal, the roar of the engine so loud it drowned out the sound of the limo's idling engine.

"I'll be right back."

She was inside, waiting in the small lounge, and the moment he saw her Ty had to force his feet to keep moving forward. As always, he wanted to stop and stare, more so today than ever before. He knew her now. Intimately. Could instantly recall the way she'd tasted, and the sound of her voice when she'd thrown her head back—

"Hey," she said, pushing herself up from the brown leather sofa. She looked momentarily uncomfortable, raising her hand to brush hair away from her face. "I didn't expect you to fetch me."

"I always escort our VIPs to meetings," he said, his voice somewhat hoarse, even to his ears. "Do you want me to take that?" he asked, motioning toward the carry-on luggage she'd brought with her.

"Uh, no. That's okay."

He turned away.

"Nice place," she said from behind him.

Harrison's Boots had been around long enough

that the company actually owned the land and had built the hangar. The building had all the amenities of a commercial airline's Admirals Club, right down to the big-screen TV, plush furniture and kitchenette in the corner for when the weather prevented guests from taking off right away.

"Thank you," Ty said, holding the glass door open for her, the heels of her boots catching on the weather stripping at the threshold. And he breathed in her scent, closing his eyes before he could stop himself.

Damn it.

"Chilly here," she said, snuggling into her sheep-skin jacket.

"It's November."

"Yes, but I always forget how cold the mountain states are."

The limo driver held open the door. Ty helped her inside, then stood for a moment in the cold afternoon air.

It didn't matter that he'd been furious with her for shoving him aside so easily. It didn't matter that he knew she would continue to keep him at a distance. He wanted her for reasons that had nothing to do with the physical and everything to do with having met a woman who, for once, challenged him and confounded him and, yes, infuriated the hell out of him from time to time.

"Help yourself to whatever you want," he said,

waving his hand at the miniature fridge and cabinets as he settled next to her in the limo.

"That's okay," she murmured.

The driver shut the door.

"Listen, Ty," she said cautiously, the tension simmering between them. "About Louisiana."

"There's nothing to discuss." He shrugged.

"Yes," she insisted, "there is. You've done a lot for me, and I'm grateful. I know that my rejection must have stung—"

No. It'd pissed him off.

"—but I hope you don't take it personally."

Take it personally? Was she insane? Of course he'd done that. He'd never had a woman brush him off so quickly.

"I hardly know you well enough to take it personally."

"Terrific," she said, lifting her chin. "I'm glad to hear that."

"How's Thumper, by the way?" he asked, keeping his eyes away from her.

"The vet expects a full recovery."

He nodded. "And you performed well this weekend?"

"I did," she said, staring out the window. Tall pines flicked shadows across the limo. "We didn't win, but we earned money."

"That's all you need to do to make it to the NFR— earn money, right?"

"The other girls will be hoping for the same thing."

"But the others don't have your talent and your dedication."

Her gaze slammed into his. "No," she said, straightening. "They don't."

He recognized her words for what they were—a clear warning that she hadn't changed her mind.

He would just have to see about that.

"Let's go over your itinerary for the day," he said, reaching for his briefcase on the floor. "We're on a tight schedule."

She leaned in close when he pulled out a sheet of paper, and Ty cursed himself for not having had Annie make two copies. The scent of Caro wafted up, and it wasn't the sweet floral he usually associated with her. No. Today she was earthy. Ty had to lean away to keep from reacting, although there was nothing he could do about the erection.

"We'll do the photo shoot first, as that's most important. We'll be doing that in our own conference room to make things easier on you. Max Arnold has shot stuff for a number of Fortune 500 companies. You'll be in good hands. After that we'll record the voice-overs for your commercial. Unfortunately, we have to go off site for that. There's only three or four lines you'll have to read. Shouldn't take more than a half hour. And after that, it's dinner."

Dinner? The words had come tumbling out of his mouth before he could dam the flow.

"I…" She met his gaze. "I had no idea this was a social visit."

He pulled the day's schedule away from her before she spotted the fact that there was no mention of a restaurant on it. "Nonetheless," he said, "it will look strange if I don't feed you tonight."

"Strange or no, I'd rather do fast food."

"And I'd rather stick to the itinerary. Harrison's Boots is your sponsor, Caroline. Don't read anything more into this than what it is."

She stiffened, her blond hair falling over her shoulders as she raised her chin. "Very well," she said. "I won't."

But the question was, would he?

Chapter Fourteen

She didn't know what she expected the headquarters of Harrison's Boots to look like, but it certainly wasn't the four-story building the limo pulled up in front of.

"At one time we occupied the whole place," Ty explained, as the two of them stepped onto the curb. Caro looked up and down Central Avenue—and felt as if she'd stepped back in time. "But we outgrew the facility after the Second World War," he continued. "So we bought an industrial building on the outskirts of town. However, our corporate offices are still here. We lease the bottom floor to speciality shops—perfect for the tourist trade."

She'd had no idea. Certainly she'd known the company had been around for awhile, but she'd had no clue just how long until now. Long, old-fashioned double-paned windows stretched across the facade.

"Here we are," he said as they stood in the shadow

of the building, before a glass door with Harrison's Boots written in gold script. A slight breeze played with her hair and she shivered. But not because of the cold.

The date stamped on the cornerstone was 1899.

"Have you always had your headquarters here?"

"Yes," Ty said, looking every inch the business-man in his black suit and dark gray tie. "Although the building didn't start out this size. My great-great-grandfather had a way with money. He'd tripled the family fortune by the time he died in 1931. We even survived the stock market crash, mostly because we make something that's never gone out of style and everyone needs—boots."

Century.

Not a single decade. Not even a few decades like most businesses had been around for. A century. Wow.

She stood in the doorway, feeling the cool air from outside racing past to the warmer interior.

Ty ran a family dynasty.

"It's a nice building," she mumbled, because truth-fully, she didn't know what else to say. It was one thing to know your sponsor was financially viable, an-other to see evidence of that success firsthand.

"Yes, it is nice. We're proud of it. Come on," he said. "We're keeping the photographer waiting."

Embarrassed, Caro felt her cheeks heat as she fol-lowed him to an antique elevator, complete with brass kick plates and wooden doors. The interior looked ultramodern, however. Ty pressed the button for the fourth floor. Caro tried to breathe, the suffocating feeling she'd begun to experience downstairs only worsening as they rose. Limos. A jet. A business that had been around for a hundred years. Who was the real Ty? The high-powered executive who ran a multimillion-dollar empire? Or the compassionate man who'd held her hand and done…other things to her?

And why did it matter?

"There she is," someone cried as the doors opened with a bang and a rush of air.

"Dad," Ty said, straightening his tall frame when he caught sight of his father.

Slim Harrison pulled away from the reception desk, his cowboy hat as battered as an old saddle. "Thought you two would never arrive."

"What are you doing here?" Ty asked him, as the pretty blonde who manned the reception desk shot them all a smile.

"That's the same thing you said to me in Louisiana, son, and it's making me think you don't want me around."

"I'm just surprised," Ty said. "You haven't been to our headquarters in—"

"A few months," Slim answered. "But you know I like to come down here from time to time, just to see how things are going."

"Indeed, I do," Ty said, his expression somewhat exasperated.

"How's Thumper?" Slim asked, as Caro realized

again how great a contrast there was between Slim and his son. Ty looked like he belonged on Wall Street. Slim, in his worn jeans and white button-down, looking like he belonged on the street below. Cowboy versus CEO. What an odd family.

"Thumper's doing better," she said with a grin. She was glad to see Slim, even if his son wasn't. "I was told the other day that his leg looks great and that the bone is healing as perfectly as they'd hoped."

"Excellent," Slim said, coming forward and placing an arm around her shoulders.

Yes, she liked Slim Harrison.

"And so now it's business as usual," the old cowboy said, nodding toward the conference room. Beyond the glass walls Caro could see photography equipment and a man who didn't look old enough to graduate from high school fiddling with a camera.

"Yup. Business as usual."

Or as usual as it could get given that she'd been intimate with Slim's son. Every time she looked Ty in the eye she found herself wondering…

Stop it.

"This must be Caroline Sheppard," said the photographer, taking her hand. Upon closer inspection, he wasn't as young as she'd thought; his short-cropped brown hair was sprinkled with gray. His brown eyes crinkled at the corners as he studied her intently. "By the looks of it, you're going to make this an easy job."

And so it began. She was given a pair of boots to wear, then told to select an outfit from one of three hanging on a rack. A quick change in a nearby bathroom and she was given over to a makeup artist.

And the whole time, Ty watched.

So did Slim and any Harrison's employees who happened to walk by. But it was Ty's eyes she felt.

We won't know until we try.

That's what he'd said to her. She hadn't realized how much she wanted to do exactly that until this very moment. Despite the rift between them, he kept sending her encouraging nods, even though they seemed forced. But he wasn't giving her the cold shoulder, and after what she'd said to him, she wouldn't have blamed him if he had.

"I think we're done here," Max said a few hours later. "And right on schedule, too."

Done? Already? That meant dinner in another...

"Great job, Caroline," Slim said.

"Caro," she corrected automatically. "Nobody but my mom calls me that."

"How is your mom, by the way?"

"Good," she said with a tip of her lips. "She wants me to come home after New Mexico."

The Dodge Circuit Finals. Her last chance to make the NFR.

Her stomach seized just thinking about it.

"You should," Slim said. "Rest up before the NFR."

And that's what touched her, Caro thought. Neither Slim nor Ty ever doubted she'd make it.

He's your sponsor, Caro. Of course he wants you to do well.

"In fact," Slim said, "I'm thinking it might be good to get a little home-cooked food in your belly before you go."

"Your son's already taking me to dinner," she said, her pulse escalating at the thought of being alone with Ty at a restaurant.

If he took her to a restaurant.

Adrenaline sent blood rushing through her body, all but draining it from her head.

"Bah," Slim was saying. "No doubt he has plans to take you to some fancy spot. You should come out to the ranch. Have dinner there."

"Dad—"

"I'd love to show you the place."

"She can't make it," Ty answered. "We're flying her back to Texas later tonight."

"So? She'll just get a later start." Slim pushed his hat back. Caro had a hard time reconciling the old cowboy with the CEO he'd been once upon a time. "Come on out," he said. "I'll have Annie arrange a car."

"Sure," she replied. "I'd love to see the ranch."

"Excellent," Slim said. "Ty, come over early. We can go through today's photos of Caro, assuming Max here can get us copies right now."

"Can do," Max said. "Just tell me which computer to use for the download."

"Are you sure you want to look at the photos tonight?" Caro asked. "I mean, I'm sure Ty has better things to do."

She said it as an out, for Ty's sake.

She should have known better.

"Actually," he said with a tight smile, "I think my father's suggestion is excellent. But there's no need to send her a car." His smile turned into something close to a smirk. "I'll take her out to the ranch myself."

She looked exhausted when he spotted her standing on the curb outside the sound studio. They still had an hour or so of daylight left and the late light turned her hair a darker blond. Pinned up, it revealed the perfect line of her jaw. But she looked like an exhausted tourist standing there with her suitcase at her feet, one who just wanted to get home. His mouth tightened. She should be taking better care of herself. She should be getting some rest.

Hard to do, buddy, with you flying her here and there.

And suddenly he felt bad about that. When he pulled to a stop in front of her, she stared warily through the window of his F-Series truck. With a whine of the electric motor, he rolled down the window, then said, "Climb on in."

She nodded, and a moment later slid in next to him.

"You look beat," he said, forcing himself to face forward and drive.

"I am tired," she admitted, sitting at the far edge of the bucket seat.

When he stopped at a light, he glanced over at her, noting the tense lines around her mouth. The way she clenched her hands in her lap. Her sagging shoulders.

"Why don't you close your eyes," he said, accelerating as the light turned green. "It's an hour's drive."

"I won't be able to sleep," she said tersely. "Tell me about your father."

"Excuse me?" he said, turning down the street that would lead to the highway on ramp.

"Your dad."

"Why?"

She shrugged. "Because earlier I kept thinking how different the two of you are. He had me howling with laughter at stories of you as a child."

"And I don't make you laugh?" He turned onto the freeway. "Don't answer that."

"I wasn't going to."

"Clever girl." And then because he was curious, "What wild and crazy tale from my youth had you laughing the hardest?" Because he hadn't heard his father tell her any stories. Then again, he'd been out of the room a lot.

She thought for a moment, then suddenly smiled. "The lemonade stand."

"Ah, yes. The lemonade stand."

He'd been ten years old and, since living on a ranch precluded any sort of high-volume lemonade sales, he'd begged his grandfather to let him go to work with him, setting up shop—if one wanted to call a folding table and a metal chair a "shop"—in front of Harrison's Boots headquarters. Things had been going great, the summer tourist trade excellent for business. He'd raised his price twice, and probably would have raised it more if it hadn't been for that cop.

"You had to admit," Ty said, "the man was out of line."

"Oh, I agree," she said. "Spoiling a child's fun wasn't very nice."

"He told me I needed a permit."

"And then ordered you to close shop," Caro finished.

"A regular Grinch." Ty glanced at the hood of his truck, where trees and overpasses reflected in the dark green finish.

"No doubt about that. Too bad he saw you throw that lemon."

Ty shot a glance at her. "He never *saw* me do a thing. All he heard was the lemon hitting his passenger window."

"Something tells me he saw lemon pulp against the glass."

Ty pasted on a self-righteous expression. "I was aiming for the garbage can."

"Tell that to the pope," she said with a glint in her eye.

His smile turned into a soft chuckle, and he relaxed his shoulders. "He had it coming."

She smiled, too, and Ty was so captivated it was all he could do to keep his attention on the road.

"Your dad told me he knew you'd make an excellent businessman when you talked your way out of a ticket."

"Yeah, assault with a lemon," he said with another laugh.

"He said, too, that if you hadn't thrown that lemon at the cop, he probably would have done the same thing."

"That didn't stop him from grounding me."

"Said he wanted to teach you that when life gave you lemons, you didn't make lemonade on a cop's car."

"A lesson I learned well that day, especially when my punishment included mucking out forty-five stalls."

She glanced over at him. "You have more than one barn?"

"Actually, we have a covered arena. The stalls are alongside it."

Her eyes widened. "Your dad told me he raises cutting horses, but for some reason I thought it would be a small operation."

"My dad do anything small? Nope. It's been his

hobby for forever. We have two arenas, one indoor, one outdoor, a foaling barn, a stallion barn—the whole shebang."

"And here I thought it was a hobby farm."

"If you call sixty-five thousand acres a hobby."

"Sixty-five…" Words apparently failed her.

"It's one of the largest cattle ranches in the country."

"I had no idea," she said, glancing out the window.

"I think there's a lot you don't know about our family," he said.

And especially me. But maybe that would change tonight.

Maybe.

Chapter Fifteen

Caro realized he was right. As they turned off the highway onto a side road, she admitted that she wanted to learn more.

She acknowledged something else, too: she couldn't wait to see where Ty had grown up.

So when they left the paved road and crossed beneath a sign that read The Rocking H Ranch, Caro leaned forward in anticipation. The tires of Ty's truck crunched on the gravel. They traveled alongside a white fence, the early evening sun tinting the green pastures a soft orange.

"How long is your driveway?" she asked a few minutes later.

"A few miles," he said.

It looked like there was nothing out here, just lots of grass and tall pines. But then they climbed a slight incline, and she could see what was on the other side.

"Welcome to the Rocking H," Ty said a moment later.

"Oh, Ty. It's beautiful."

In a secluded valley below, horses frolicked in lush pastures. Green fields stretched all the way to the base of some low-lying mountains, with the same white fencing crisscrossing the land in a checkerboard pattern. To the left stood a large house, and beyond that a covered arena. The place looked to Caro like a Kentucky horse farm, dotted as it was with other barns and outbuildings.

"My dad won't be here for a few more minutes. Did you want to have a look around?" Ty asked as he pulled to a stop at the end of a curving drive.

"Sure." She slipped out, and found the air had grown chillier now that the sun had almost disappeared. Caro shivered, her gaze roving over the house. Two stories tall, it had bow windows that jutted out from the front. Stained glass panels framed the massive oak door, and Caro absolutely knew that inside it would smell like beeswax and lemons.

Just like home.

"Follow me."

He walked ahead and she was forced to take a couple of running steps to catch up. In his faded jeans and button-down top he looked more a cowboy today. She liked that.

Horses nickered as they approached a large structure that seemed to be not just a barn, but a second covered arena, judging by its size. Ty slid open a big wooden door, and Caro let loose a gasp when she saw what was on the other side. Beneath a massively high roof sprawled an arena the size of a football field. Fluorescent lights illuminated the sandy floor, which was furrowed with loopy patterns left by a harrow. Aluminum pipe panels surrounded the arena, and running up and down both sides were wooden stalls. Caro couldn't see the animals inside—their heads were hidden by vertical bars—but judging by the size of the operation she would bet the horses of the Rocking H Ranch were some of the best in the nation.

"You must be selling a lot of boots," she muttered.

"The horses pay for themselves," he said. "Or so I'm told."

They probably did. The cutting horse industry had some of the largest purses around, sometimes in the millions. "So you're not involved with the ranch?"

"I used to be. Now I don't have the time."

"Wow," she said, noticing a brass plaque on the door, with the name Lena's San Peppy in black letters. San Peppy. The name was legendary among quarter horses, and this pretty girl, she thought, must be a direct descendent, evidenced by the three generations of lineage posted beneath the name. "You must have some nice horses."

"My dad tells me the same thing."

A rooster crowed as she peeked into the next stall. "Oh, my," she said, staring at the gelding inside, a two-year-old by the looks of it. They bedded their horses in shavings, and the pine scent tickled her nose. The colt's hooves rustled the wood chips before he pressed his mouth against the metal bars.

"He's one of my favorites," Ty said.

She glanced up at him, curious to find out just how much he knew about horses. "What makes you say that?"

"He's put together nicely," Ty explained. "He's already got big shoulders, which more than likely means he'll be athletic. His back end is powerful, too. Pretty head, not that that really matters in the cutting horse industry, but it might come in handy if we ever put him out to stud. Breeders like fancy-looking horses."

Okay, so maybe horses were more to him than a way to gather up cattle.

"Can I go in?"

"I don't see why not," he said.

The metal pin used to keep the door from sliding open felt like ice in her hands. She pulled it free, then let it dangle from its chain. The door slid open easily, and the young colt raised his head when he realized she was coming in.

"Easy there, boy," she said gently.

The colt blew through its nose, the snort sounding like a sneeze. His sides expanded as he inhaled.

"Easy," she repeated.

It was obvious the colt was ground broke, because he dropped his head, taking a step toward her a moment later. "Silly," she said, when he butted her with his nose, "I don't have any treats in my pockets, if that's what you're looking for."

"He probably is."

Caro looked up, her heart thudding against her ribs when she saw that Ty had followed her inside. He turned and closed the door. Despite her sudden anxiety, she couldn't help but think that he seemed right at home. In his dark gray Carthart and cowboy hat, he reminded her of her brother in some respects. Except Rand didn't own a private jet. Or run a multimillion-dollar company.

"He sure is friendly."

"My father. He spoils them."

"Evidently," she said, scratching the fuzzy mane.

The colt bolted, and Caro jumped back.

Right into Ty's arms.

But he was already moving away from her, toward the animal. "It's all right," he murmured. "You're okay, Gambler."

She watched as, with a gentle hand, Ty brought the horse under control. He slipped an arm over the gelding's neck, using his other hand to scratch behind the ear. The colt appeared to like that, lowering his head and sticking out his upper lip.

"You love horses."

"I do," he admitted.

"I guess I should have known," she murmured, remembering the way he'd reacted to Thumper's injury.

He let Gambler go. "Guess you should have known what?"

"That you love horses as much as I do."

"Didn't you?"

She had. Just as she'd known he was kind and caring and thoughtful long before he'd been so kind to her and Thumper.

"I guess I did," she breathed.

"Just as you know this thing between us isn't going to go away."

"What are you doing?" she asked, when he closed the distance between them.

"You know that, too."

"Ty, I—"

He touched her lower lip. She told herself to move. But it was back again. That dizzying, somewhat terrifying sensation—the one she felt all the way to the bottom of her stomach whenever he touched her.

She was falling for him.

"Please," she said as he traced the line of her jaw with his finger.

"Please what?"

"Please don't."

"Don't stop touching you?" he asked, as he started to lower his head.

"No...I mean yes."

"I like no, don't stop touching you better," he said, and then his lips were covering hers.

She closed her eyes and let him kiss her. What

would it hurt to let him do so? What did it matter if, just for a moment she imagined that there was no plane to catch back to New Mexico, no NFR?

His mouth opened. His warmth seeped into her. Molasses and honey—that's what he tasted like.

He pressed her up against the stall. She clutched at his arms, enjoying the strength of the muscles she felt there. He reached lower, his fingers skating along the small of her back, then cupping her rear, pulling her toward—

Another rooster crowed. And they sprang apart.

Caro all but ran from the barn.

"Damn it," Ty muttered, turning his back to the stall door. From the corner, Gambler gazed at him. Ty moved to the horse, his hand shaking as he stroked the smooth coat.

"Damn," he said again, deciding he'd better follow.

His dad was unloading groceries from the back of his dark blue truck, his expression quizzical. "What'd you do to Caroline?" he asked. "She looked like a spooked calf a moment ago."

"Where is she?"

"In the house." His dad set the bag of groceries on his tailgate. "I told her to make herself at home."

"I'll go talk to her."

"Ty, wait," Slim said. "What's going on between you and that young lady? I know you told me earlier it was nothing, but I don't buy that."

"It is nothing, Dad." Ty ran a hand through his hair. "At least if Caro has her way," he added under his breath.

"You seeing each other?"

"No," Ty snarled.

His dad rested an arm on the truck, his eyes barely visible beneath the brim of his hat. Ty braced himself for the third degree that was surely coming.

"You like her?"

"Maybe."

Slim straightened and gave him that look. Ty hadn't been on the receiving end of one of those in years. And it still had the power to make him feel like a naughty little boy. Same look his dad gave him after he'd thrown the lemon at that cop.

"You *like* that woman," Slim said. It wasn't a question. "So why didn't she look happy about you kissing her in the barn?"

Kissing—

Not much got past his dad.

"She's doesn't want a relationship. Not now. She's consumed with making the NFR," Ty admitted.

"So. What about after?"

"I think she's afraid of letting her guard down."

"Why?"

"She had a bad relationship. She's gun-shy now. Before today, I hadn't spoken to her since Louisiana."

"So you flew her here as a way of breaking the ice."

Had he done that? Truthfully, they'd needed to do the photo shoot and the voice-over, the sooner, the better. Still, he could have let someone else handle the matter.

"I think so."

His dad nodded, staring out at the pastures. The sun was almost down and in the dusk, the horses' coats appeared dark brown.

"But now you're not so certain what you should do."

"I'm not," Ty confirmed. This was twice now he and his father had discussed personal matters. They hadn't talked like this since before his mom died.

"Son," Slim said, tipping back his hat, "I know you understand what can happen when you mix business with pleasure, so I'm not going to lecture you on that. Besides, I think Caroline has enough sense not to behave irrationally like that last woman. So the way I see it, you have two choices. You either bust the barrier on the way out of the gate and try to rope Caroline, or you let her get away."

"But if I decide to pursue her now, while she's trying for the NFR, I might distract her. That's already happened once before."

"What do you mean?" Slim asked, squinting against the last rays of the sun.

"I think I'm partly to blame for Thumper's injury. She said she didn't warm him up properly because of me."

"Hogwash," Slim said with a dismissive wave. "What happened to Thumper was a freak accident. He moved wrong when he bucked or something. Maybe even clipped himself with his own back hoof. It could have happened at any time and anywhere."

"You think so?" Ty asked, feeling some of the weight he'd been carrying lifted off his shoulders.

"I'm certain of it."

"But I still hate to pursue her while she's so focused on the NFR."

"Then wait a bit," Slim said. "Give her some space."

I don't want to wait.

When he wanted something, he always went after it.

"You look undecided," Slim said.

"I am."

His dad nodded, hefted a paper bag. Ty thought their conversation over when his father turned away. But after taking a step, the older man spun back, crinkling the bag in his arms.

"Look, son. You know I've never been one to interfere in your love life—we've never been that close—but I think you should take a long, hard look at yourself and your feelings for this woman. I see something when the two of you are together, something you guys probably don't even see yourself."

"What?"

"You bring each other to life. I see a spark in your

eyes. I hear it in your voice, too. The reason I flew down to Louisiana was to see for myself if what I suspected was true."

"And what's that?"

Slim shifted the bags in his arms. "If you were finally starting to come alive again."

Ty stiffened.

"If you were finally ready to open your heart again. Love isn't always pretty. For better or worse, they say. Sometimes that worse is pretty bad, like your mom's death."

"Dad—"

"No, let me finish. I don't think you realize how much you've closed yourself off. I know your mom's death affected you deeply, but it's nearly killed me to see you and I drift further apart. If this woman makes you feel things, then it's an answer to my prayer. Don't let her put you off."

"Dad," Ty said as his father started to walk away again.

Slim glanced back.

"Thanks."

Slim nodded.

Chapter Sixteen

Caro knew they'd been talking about her the moment Slim and Ty walked into the remodeled farmhouse. She cautiously got up from the claw-foot sofa. The room's soaring ceilings made her feel small and alone.

"You ready for some dinner?" Slim asked.

Caro nodded, and though she tried to avoid eye contact, she somehow found Ty's eyes.

This thing between us won't go away.

All it had taken was one kiss for Caro to admit defeat. And if he could turn her head that easily, she would need to watch herself in the future.

"Come on into the kitchen," Slim said. "We're not big on formal here."

It was like that at her mom's house, Caro thought. She followed them across the creaking wood floors. Caro was completely enchanted with the house's crown molding, wainscoted walls and airy floor plan.

"This is beautiful," she exclaimed, her hand on an antique side table.

"Yup," Slim said. "We love this old house. Ty's got a place a few miles away, not that he spends a lot of time there."

"No?"

"He has a condo back in town," Slim said. "Makes it easier on late nights."

"I see," she said, settling into a chair that'd been tucked under an old oak table, one that looked as if it'd been refinished and restained a dozen times.

"We've added to the place over the years," Slim said, setting the groceries on the counter. "This kitchen is still pretty much the same, though. Well, aside from the cabinets being redone."

"Who's cooking?" she asked.

"We both are," Slim answered, taking out a package. "Hope you like apple pie filling."

"I do. Why?"

"We like to cook pork with it."

"Really?"

"Yup," Slim said.

She couldn't believe the Harrisons were cooking for her.

"It's delicious," she said an hour later, savoring the first bite. Not only did they slather pie filling and brown sugar over the top, they'd spread stuffing beneath it—the combination of flavors were divine.

"It was my mom's favorite dish," Ty said.

They were the first words he'd said directly to her since their episode in the barn. Slim had been holding up the conversation.

"She had good taste," Caro said, resolving to ask for the recipe. Her mom would love to serve such a yummy meal to guests at her family's dude ranch.

"Yes, she did," Slim agreed. "Though she wasn't always happy with my concoctions." He launched into a story about the jalapeño chicken he'd once cooked up.

The rest of their conversation flowed as easily, despite the tension between Ty and herself. As Caro looked from father to son, she realized she really liked them. And she would have enjoyed spending more time with them.

If she'd *had* the time.

As if to punctuate the thought, Ty said, "Dad, as much as I know you'd enjoy sitting here telling Caro all my deep, dark secrets, she has to go. She has horses to ride in the morning."

Yes, she did. And she'd get to them on a private jet. Sure, her family had money, but not like the Harrisons. It intimidated her, even though she told herself she was being ridiculous.

"Aww," Slim said, "that's too bad. I was enjoying myself."

She'd enjoyed herself, too. Perhaps more than she should have.

"Your dad's great," she said after they'd left.

"He likes you."

"Really?"

Ty nodded. Now that they were alone, it seemed he felt no need to talk. Not after he helped her into the truck, and not once he started driving back to the airport. That was good, because, frankly, she didn't know what to say. She liked Ty, but there were too many impediments in their way.

But she *liked* him.

And *he* liked *her.*

She could see it in his eyes as he helped her out of his truck.

"Thank you," she said, still not quite able to process that she was about to be whisked back to her horses in his private jet. "I had a really good time."

Despite what had happened in the barn.

"We did, too."

Would he try to kiss her? She thought he might, even saw him lean toward her.

But the next moment he stepped back, and Caro knew he was trying to give her space.

"I'll see you," she said softly.

"See you," he repeated, tucking his hands in his pockets.

Caro tensed with every step she took toward the plane.

Kiss me. Kiss me. Kiss me.

Damn her stupid heart, she really, truly wanted that.

She heard his car start before she'd reached the

jet, where the pilot who'd flown her to Wyoming was waiting.

"Ready?" he asked.

No. Not at all. "Ready," she said.

Caro tried to focus when she arrived in New Mexico. She really did. But it was fruitless to try to banish Ty from her mind.

She was almost grateful when the day for her to compete arrived at last. Soon she would know if she was going to ride in the NFR. The odds were slim, but she had a chance.

"All right, girl," she said, mounting Classy, the overhead lights in the holding area bleaching her chestnut's coat to palomino. "Let's see what you can do."

She entered the huge structure, both she and her horse blinking against the brightness inside. There was a practice arena in one corner, the ever-present concrete walls keeping the sound of the crowd at bay.

He wasn't there.

She hadn't expected Ty to show up. Of course not. And yet it appeared there was still a small part of her hoping…

Dumb.

"Good luck tonight, Caro," someone called. Caro looked up. Melanie, one of the other girls with a shot at making it, waved to her.

"You, too, Mel."

Steer wrestlers and team ropers mixed with barrel racers, the women who were running tonight all wearing their most sparkling shirts. Caro wore gold. It looked beautiful with Classy's coloring. The saddle pad was new, too, with Harrison's Boots inscribed on a piece of leather near the corner.

"You ready?" the gate man asked.

"I am," Caro said. But was she really? Her hands shook, a fact she tried to hide by clutching the reins.

"Have a safe ride," the guy said when it was her turn to go.

She winced. But she refused to let the reminder of what happened to Thumper affect her now. Not tonight. "Thanks," she said, clucking her horse into a trot.

Someone blazed past them. Jenna Thomas, Caro noticed, and her run must have been a good one judging by how fast she blew by both her and Terri.

Classy barely lifted her head.

"You can wake up now," she told the mare.

"Must be nice," the woman on deck said. She was having a heck of a time keeping her own horse calm. Usually Caro was too busy trying to control Thumper to pay attention to who was after her. Tonight she was able to turn around and say, "I think maybe I need a cattle prod."

"I think you're right."

"All right, let's go," she told the mare, kicking her horse forward. The mare eased into a lope. Caro almost laughed. Classy was acting like a plow horse.

Sure, her ears were pricked forward. Undoubtedly she could hear the crowd inside the arena. But she didn't balk or shy or hollow her back. She just loped along. When Caro told her to go faster, she barely picked up speed.

Caro giggled.

Okay, so she wouldn't get killed. She'd be lucky to make it around the barrels in the allotted seconds. But that was okay. Plenty of time to teach Classy how to—

Caro's laughter turned to a gasp of surprise. It was as if the mare had been waiting for just the right moment. All of a sudden Caro was on a rocket ship, her reins and saddle flapping in rhythm to Classy's thundering feet.

"Wow," she said. "All righty then. Let's go."

She pointed Classy toward the first barrel. The mare never hesitated.

Not bad. We might be able to do this. Just slow down, Classy. Not much, just a touch...

Around they went.

Caro gunned it. The mare responded. Next barrel, across the short end of the arena. Classy headed right for it. Caro braced herself, waited for the moment Classy realized there was a boatload of people watching them perform. But the mare didn't seem to care. Lowering her head, she bent her body around the second barrel. Caro had to grab the saddle horn to stay on.

"Holy—"

She grinned, her smile so wide she was certain people watching at home could see her white teeth.

"Easy…" This run was longer, the barrel at the far end of the arena. They'd be moving at top speed, which meant they needed to be careful, needed to time things perfectly. "Just a touch slower—"

Classy lowered her head. Her left leg thrust out farther than the right as she rounded the last barrel. One stride, two.

Done!

The crowd went wild. Caro could hear their roar, worried for a moment that Classy might get frightened. But her little horse just kept on running, galloping toward the electronic timers as if she'd done it a hundred times.

"Whoo-hee," the announcer said. "That was one smokin' run. Let's see if she can—"

Caro heard him yell "Yes!" as she exited the arena. "That's fast time, ladies and gentlemen. We'll have to wait and see if it'll hold up, but so far there's your leader."

Caro collapsed onto Classy's neck. The mare must have taken it as a cue to slow down. Either that or she'd run out of steam.

"Wow," one of her fellow competitors said. "That was quite a run."

Caro grinned. "I had no idea she had that in her."

"Looks like you won't need to worry about making it to the NFR."

The NFR.

Cripes. She'd forgotten.

"Yeah, but we won't know until later tonight. After they post the final money."

"Right," the redhead said. "But you've got a shot."

Did she?

It was the longest wait of her life, but when the PRCA official handed her the list, Caro could tell by his wide grin that she was in.

"Congratulations," he said.

"What?" she screamed, causing a few heads outside the show office to turn.

"You're in."

She didn't know the man, but she hugged him as if he was her best friend. But as he hugged her back, she wished it was another man.

She wished it was Ty.

Chapter Seventeen

The next morning her cell phone was still ringing. And it wasn't just friends and family who were calling, it was the media, too. Suddenly, she was a hot commodity. Her horse, Classy, was an equine Cinderella story, what with Thumper breaking his leg and then this unknown stepping in so brilliantly. The network broadcasting the finals wanted to do a feature. They'd asked if they could go with her when she went back to California for a brief rest before the finals.

Back home.

Never before had Caro longed so much for the peace and quiet of her childhood. She needed time to sit back, to analyze everything that had happened.

To figure out what to do about Ty.

He'd left her a message. Congratulated her. She'd heard his voice and wished...

But that was silly. Now more than ever she needed

to focus. She had a horse capable of running well. If she could just do it again! Because Caro couldn't escape one fact: it might have been a fluke. Classy might only have one good run in her. There was every possibility that when they got to Las Vegas the mare would freak out. Sometimes that happened. Sometimes a horse took an instant dislike to a place. Classy might do just that.

But did it matter?

They'd made it to the NFR, Caro thought, banging her hands on the steering wheel. The freakin' NFR!

It was a long drive home. But that was okay. Driving gave her time to think. And to brood, because it dawned on her that winning in New Mexico was a double-edged sword. Now that she'd made it to the NFR she'd have to see Ty again in Las Vegas. He'd want to attend. Of course he'd want to be there. She'd have to be near him, and that might mess with her mind.

Pulling into the Diamond W was bittersweet. The last time she'd been home had been for her father's memorial. The house had been full of people, the long driveway lined with cars. But now there were only trucks parked in front of the four-story ranch house that doubled as the main quarters for the Diamond W Dude Ranch. No one even came outside to greet her as she slowly made the left-hand turn at the bottom of the horseshoe-shaped driveway. That was strange.

She pulled her rig past the main house, trying to catch a glimpse through the tall windows behind the wraparound porch. No one. Even more strange. Normally you'd find a guest or two milling about, but the place seemed deserted.

The barn looked deserted, too. She'd talked to her mom earlier that day, so she knew Caro was coming. She'd even told Caro she'd have two stalls ready for Classy and her other horse to bed down in. When Caro got out, she went in search of those stalls, walking up to the huge old barn which had grayed with age. The doors swung open instead of sliding as they did on modern barns, so she always felt as if she were going into a castle.

"Surprise!"

Caro just about jumped out of her cowboy boots as she stared into the barn. Dozens of people smiled at her, holding signs that said things like, NFR, Here We Come, Do You Know the Way to Las Vegas or Vegas or Bust. Caro stood and stared, then covered her face with her hands and choked back a laugh. Rand was there. So was her other brother, Nick. Flora and Edith, two of her mom's closest friends, were there as well, along with Amanda and Scott Sheppard. And Lani and Chase Cavenaugh. The whole gang.

"Well, look what the cat dragged in," Chase called, his battered straw hat tipped back on his head. "A bona fide rodeo star."

"And a beautiful one at that," said Lani, his wife. "Who's going to be the first to give her a hug?"

Half-a-dozen male voices cried out, "I will," which made everyone laugh, and then suddenly Caro was enveloped by friends. Every rancher within fifty miles must have come out to greet her. "Where the heck did you hide the cars?" she asked.

"They're out in the south pasture," her mom said, the first to give her a hug. "And boy, are the cows mad."

Caro laughed through her tears. She only wished her dad were here to share this.

And then there was Ty. And Slim.

"Surprise," he said.

"This *is* a surprise," she told Ty's father. Ty hugged her next.

"What are you doing here?" she asked, a bit more sharply than she intended.

"You didn't think I'd give up on us that easily, did you?"

She inhaled, prepared to put him in his place, but she couldn't. She was just too damn happy to see him.

"No," she said softly. "I really didn't."

He smiled, but she noticed he didn't pull her to him. He was giving her space, and she appreciated that more than he would ever know.

"Come on," she said to both Ty and Slim. "I'll introduce you to the gang."

"In a sec. First I want to give you this." Ty held out a DVD case.

"What's this?"

"Your commercial."

She glanced up at him. "Wow."

He handed it to her. "Congratulations."

"Thanks."

"And good luck," he said, turning.

"Wait," she said, shooting Slim a helpless glance. "You're leaving?"

"I am."

"But,..you just got here, didn't you? And you flew all the way from Wyoming."

Slim frowned, but he didn't try to persuade Ty to stay. He must know what's going on, Caro thought.

"I only came because your mom insisted."

Her mother. She glanced to where her mom stood. She was watching them with eagle eyes.

"She made it sound as if she'd be insulted if I missed this."

"She's skilled at that," Caro said, shaking her head. Her mom was the queen of matchmaking, and it didn't take a genius to figure out why she'd wanted Ty on the ranch so badly.

"My dad wants to stay, though. You can introduce him around."

"But—"

"I'll see you at the NFR."

"Yeah. The NFR."

"Good luck," he said, his eyes intense.

"Thanks."

He'd left because he couldn't stand to be near her and not *be* with her. But walking away was one of the hardest things he'd ever done.

Damn it.

He headed for his car, but was so distracted he took a wrong turn and found himself at the edge of a lake. It was late afternoon and the place was deep in shadows, and the sunlight barely visible through the treetops. If he hadn't been in such a hurry to leave, he'd have stopped and enjoyed the stillness for a while. Instead he turned to retrace his steps.

And there she was.

Ty had to clasp his hands to keep from reaching for her, pulling her to him.

"I don't want you to leave."

He stiffened, his heart thumping against his chest.

"I missed you in New Mexico. I didn't realize how much until seeing you now," she said. "When I was waiting for the results, I kept wanting to call you."

"You told me to stay away."

"I know. And I really wanted you to…until you weren't there."

His pulse quickened. "What are you saying, Caro?"

"I don't know what I'm saying," she admitted, looking out over the lake. Her hair was down, loose around her shoulders—his favorite style. He wanted to run his fingers through it.

"I don't know what it means. I just know that for some strange reason, after I won my event, and then qualified for the NFR, I wanted you there. With me."

He watched her. Emotions played across her face. He recognized one of them, and it prompted him to finally touch her hand. "You don't have to do this alone."

"I know," she said quietly. "The question is, do I want to do it with you?"

"There's one way to find out."

Her eyes looked as blue as the lake beyond. "I know."

Ty's breathing grew even more shallow when he saw what was in her eyes.

"Kiss me," she said softly.

"Are you certain?" he murmured.

"As certain as I'll ever be."

He leaned toward her. Caroline told herself it wasn't too late. That she could pull back. Run away.

She didn't.

"Caroline," he said, her name a whisper against her lips.

She closed her eyes. She loved when he called her that. It made her feel sexy. Womanly. *Desirable.*

"Ty."

Their mouths opened the moment their lips touched. His taste filled her mouth—like mint and coffee. And something else, fruity and sweet. It took her a moment to realize that was his own, unique flavor.

Ty.

She wanted more. They might be out in the open. Heck, there might even be some of her mom's guests watching them through windows, but Caro didn't care. She wanted him.

He lifted his hand, touched her breasts. She arched into him. The last time he'd touched her there, he'd felt bare skin. She wanted that again, so much that she pushed her hand between them, cupping him.

"Caroline," he said softly. "Don't do that unless you don't want this to end."

"Maybe I don't," she said, stroking him.

"Jeez," he gasped.

"Let's go," she said, tired of waiting.

"You know what will happen if I come with you."

"I know," she said, taking his hand.

She led him up to the main house, to one of her mom's private guest bedrooms, the place deserted because of her party.

A party she'd miss out on. But she didn't care.

"Are you sure?" he asked, when they stood outside the bedroom door.

She kissed him again. He scooped her up, and the next minute they were falling onto the bed, her legs wrapped around his waist. She felt his masculine heat, and knew this time she wanted it all.

She pulled at his shirt, undoing a button here, a jean snap there. She heard someone moan. Was it her? She didn't know. She tingled and burned in anticipation of his touch. His sweet, intimate touch.

Cool air brushed her skin. She let him part her shirt, then pull it from her waistband. He shucked off his before landing half on top of her, reaching for her breasts. Where had her bra gone? She didn't remember taking it off, but she didn't care, because he was suckling at her breasts and she was moaning and her jeans were being pulled down and she could feel the coarse hair of his legs brush against the smooth curves of her calves.

Naked.

They were both naked and he was moving down her body, dropping kisses against each rib, her muscles contracting when he licked her belly. He used one hand to part her legs.

"Yes," she heard herself moan. "Please. Yes."

She wanted him to kiss her there again. It had been so good the other night. Surely it couldn't be that way again.

But she wanted to find out.

She felt his hot breath first, then his tongue and, yes. Oh, yes. It was as good as before. Maybe better.

"There," she urged him, glancing down and watching the top of his head as he licked and sucked and did things to her that made her arch and tense. Her body began to tighten. She knew she was close, but he seemed to know that, too. Perhaps he'd learned his lesson the first time, because he pulled away at the last minute, leaving Caro pleased yet disappointed that he'd read her so well.

"Ty," she cried out.

"Wait," he rasped, kissing the insides of her thighs. "Just wait."

But she didn't want to wait. She wanted it now.

Her body seemed to have taken on a life of its own. Her limbs felt heavy, as if someone held them down. She burned, but at the same time sprouted goose bumps, chilled now that he was moving up her body. She could feel his manhood brush against her thighs, and she pulled her legs up, welcoming him.

But he moved higher, offering himself to her. "Touch me," he said.

She wanted to do more than touch him; she wanted to lap at him like he'd done to her. But he didn't seem to want that, because when she urged him closer, he resisted.

She clasped him with her hand.

"Caro."

Her body pulsed in response to that low-throated moan. She understood then. He didn't want it to end, either. He wanted her to tease him, as he'd teased her. He wanted them both to enjoy every throbbing sensation. She understood and she played the game, running her hand up and down the length of him.

"Don't think I can take it much longer," he groaned.

No. She didn't think she could, either. There was a buzzing in her ears, and her body trembled so badly it was all she could do to keep her hand steady.

He touched her.

She almost slipped over the edge. She felt her abdominal muscles contract, knew her climax was near, felt a momentary disappointment because she wanted to keep it all going…

He touched her again.

"Ty," she cried.

His body slid down hers. She knew what he would do next, and lifted her hips in anticipation. His gaze met her own. It was a moment out of time, one they would never forget, the infinitesimal pause before their bodies joined. For the first time.

His lips closed over hers at the same moment he entered her. He caught her groan with his mouth. She felt his tongue against hers, just as he plunged deep.

Oh, God.

She couldn't take it anymore. Couldn't hold on…

"Ty."

Her body tightened, then tightened even more.

Release.

Each pleasure-filled wave made her moan.

He seemed to be waiting for that, because when she looked into his eyes, she saw satisfaction there. And then his face went slack as he pushed into her.

Hearts pounding, slick with sweat, the two of them clutched each other as, for the first time, they understood what it meant to truly be with someone not just physically, but emotionally, too.

Chapter Eighteen

Ty couldn't take his eyes off her as she slept. It was late, the party probably long since over. He wondered if any of the guests had worried about what happened to them. But of course they would figure it out. Like his father said, the way he and Caro stared at each other had to be obvious to the whole world.

And she'd be leaving soon.

"Caro," he whispered, not wanting to give her up.

She stirred, smiled in her sleep—turned toward him.

"Caro," he said again, dropping kisses on her cheek, first the right one, then the left.

"Ty," she said softly, opening her eyes.

His heart stopped. That's what it seemed like.

"Hi," he murmured, kissing her near her ear.

"What time is it?" she asked, glancing at the clock.

"Not even midnight," he said. "I'm hungry.

Thought maybe you were hungry, too. Want me to get you something?"

"Gosh," she said, pushing her hair away from her face. "I suppose I am. I never ate at the party."

"They're probably all wondering where we ran off to."

"Oh, I think they know."

"Yeah. They probably do," he said with a slight smile. He felt a lump growing in his throat. "You want to raid the refrigerator with me?"

"I'm game for anything," she said, smiling.

Something about her smile always did it for him. Even watching her get dressed filled him with a sense of wonder. How had they reached this point? More important, would she stay?

The question plagued him as they sneaked through the halls. He couldn't seem to stop touching her.

"When do you have to leave for the NFR?"

"Next week," she said. "Probably Monday. I'll want to get there early so Classy can settle in."

"You want company?"

She stopped in the middle of the hallway, a night-light near the floor illuminating her face. "You're not thinking of going to the NFR, are you?"

"Of course," he said, peering down at her. There was just enough light to see into her eyes. "Harrison's Boots is your sponsor. We have a suite that we'll expect you to visit from time to time. We have several

VIPs who'd like to meet you, too. The media will be in and out, too. We've even hired a PR firm to help you manage your schedule and, judging by the number of calls you've received, I suspect you'll need them."

"I can't have you at the NFR."

He took a step back. "What?"

"Ty, I told you weeks ago. It's too...distracting when you're around." She shook her head. "I can't concentrate."

"Yeah, but that was before."

"Nothing's changed," she said, hugging her jacket closer.

"Yes, Caro, it has," he said, shifting on the plush carpet. "We've been intimate. You can't just expect me to slink away as if nothing has happened."

"No one's asking you to *slink*," she said, loudly enough to wake anyone nearby. She lowered her voice. "I'm just saying I'd rather you not be there."

"Don't be ridiculous."

"This isn't a request, Ty," she said, pulling back. "I'm telling you, please, if you have any respect for me as a barrel racer, you'll steer clear and allow me to focus."

"Of course I have respect for that, but you can't expect me to hide every time you come near."

"No," she said with what he thought was a small laugh. "I don't expect that. Just leave me alone until after the NFR. If I see you in the suite, fine—that's different. But I can't have you hanging around before a performance. You'll get in my way. Ruin my concentration."

Ty tried to hide his frustration. He knew she was right, damn it all, remembering Thumper. Despite what his dad said, he still worried about that happening again. But that didn't make it any easier to bear. "At least I'll have you to myself for the rest of the week."

"What do you mean? I thought you were going home." Her eyes looked even bigger and wider in the late hour.

"I can take a week off."

She began to seem panicked. "But…I have things to do. I have to prepare. Classy needs to be exercised."

"Not every hour of every day."

Behind him, or perhaps downstairs, he could hear voices. "Caro, what's really the issue here?"

"What? There's no issue."

"Yes, there is. One minute we're in there—" he motioned to the room down the hall "—making love, and the next you're dismissing me."

"I'm not dismissing you." The people down below stopped talking. "I told you last week I wouldn't be able to spend time with you until after the NFR."

"You can't control the whole world, Caro."

"What? This isn't about controlling the world."

"You think if you can keep me out of sight, I'll be out of your mind. But love doesn't work that way."

"Love?"

"Isn't that where this is going?"

Love. Was he saying he was in love with her? He couldn't be. It was too soon for that. They'd only just met. "Ty," she said. "I'm not sure where this is going, but it's late. And I'm tired. And hungry."

"We need to talk about this tonight, Caro, because I'm not going back to that bedroom with you. I'm not going to hold you, to make love to you, if all I am to you is a way to let off some steam."

"That's a low blow," she said softly, her heart beating so rapidly she could feel the pulse at her temples.

"This isn't a fling for me, Caro—"

"I never said it was for me," she interjected.

"Then why are you treating it like one?"

"I'm not. After the NFR—"

"No."

"Excuse me?"

"If this isn't just a fling to you, Caro—if this is something special and unique—then I should be there for you. It might take some getting used to on your part, but it won't be as hard as you think. Not if this was meant to be."

Meant to be?

That sounded an awful lot like a declaration of

love. "It's too soon, Ty. You're asking too much. I can't commit to anything right now."

"Right now, Caro? Or ever?"

She thought for a moment. It was all happening too fast. "I don't know."

"Good night, Caro."

"Where are you going?" she called after him.

"I'm not sure. To find a hotel, I guess."

"Ty," she said, following. "Don't. Let's talk about this."

"Why? So you can brush me off at the NFR?"

"I wouldn't just brush you off."

"Then let me be a part of this. From here on out. Starting now. Let me show you this can work."

She didn't move. Her pulse began to race even more.

"You won't let me, will you, Caro?"

"Ty…"

"I'll see you around," he said, bending and giving her a kiss on the cheek. "Good luck at the NFR."

She didn't follow when he walked away.

Chapter Nineteen

She told herself they would work things out. That she'd see Ty the next morning. But when she went down to breakfast, he was gone.

"So he really did leave?" she asked Slim, the smell of bacon filling the air.

"Yup. He took off," the old cowboy said, lifting the lid on one of the chafing dishes. They were in the dining room, with most of the chairs tucked into the long table behind them, empty. "Left at the crack of dawn."

After their argument.

"Did he say when he'd be back?"

"He told me to tell you he'd see you around. Maybe at the NFR."

The room was bright with early morning sunlight. Then why did it feel as if a shadow had just fallen over her?

"He didn't do something wrong, did he?" Slim asked.

Ty's father looked different without his cowboy hat. Younger, maybe. Or maybe that was because she could see he had a full head of gray hair.

"No," she said. "He hasn't done anything wrong."

"Good. Because if he took advantage of you last night, only to leave you high and dry, I'll paddle his bottom."

Caro blushed. Did Slim know she'd left the party to be with his son?

Obviously, he did, judging by the way he studied her face. "No need to do that," she said with a weak smile. "I just…didn't think he was leaving quite so soon."

"Join the club," Slim said. "When I saw you two sneaking up to the house, I thought…"

He'd seen that?

"Well, doesn't matter what I thought. You want to sit down and eat some breakfast with me?"

She wasn't hungry all of a sudden. "I don't think so."

"You sure?"

"No. That's okay." She patted her stomach. "I think I'm nervous about next week."

Slim studied her even more carefully. Caro looked away. She had a feeling the wise old guy saw too much.

"When are you leaving?"

"Think I'll stick around a few days," he said.

She nodded. "I'll see you later then."

"Caro," he said as she turned away. "This may be none of my business, but if you and Ty had a fight…"

"No, no. It's nothing like that."

They'd just broken up. No big deal. They hadn't known each other long enough for it to matter.

Right, Caro?

To her horror, tears began to fall. "I've got to go," she said, ducking out of the room.

Slim watched her escape. "Love," he said. "These young kids don't know a thing about it."

She arrived at University Nevada Las Vegas the following Tuesday, with plenty of time to get Classy settled in before their first performance on Saturday. The days flew by fast. There was a lot to see and do at the NFR. Exhibits, arts and crafts, clothing booths—you name it, it was there. That's how Caro kept herself busy in between exercising Classy. When she was through at night, she fell asleep exhausted.

But not so exhausted that she didn't dream about Ty.

That was a ridiculous thing to have happen, she told herself. They'd been intimate once. Well, twice. Sort of. But that's all it'd been—physical.

Except she still dreamed of him, and sometimes all they were doing in her dreams was having a conversation. Sometimes she woke up with the memory of his look—the intense stare that always made her self-conscious and nervous and excited all at once.

So perhaps she wasn't quite at the top of her game that first day of competition, but she was close. She'd get eight other tries after this, the person with the highest average winning the coveted title of World Champion. No matter what happened, there was always tomorrow.

Her only distraction was her own mind, but when she kept busy she could stay focused. And that's what she did all morning. She groomed Classy until her coat shone. Combed out her mane until it looked as soft as cotton. Clipped her legs and her ears as if they were headed for the show pen instead of a rodeo ring. By the time Caro was ready to saddle up, she felt reasonably calm. Classy had been a dream all week, and Caro was starting to think—albeit cautiously—she might have a shot.

It went terribly wrong from the start.

The stalls were outside, as at most venues. But this was Las Vegas in December, and by the time the evening performance started, it was cold. And windy. Every rider knew to use caution on a windy day. But what choice did Caro have? So she mounted up. Classy immediately began to buck and snort. Caro was so taken by surprise she nearly came off. Two bucks later, she had Classy under control.

"Ride 'em, cowgirl," Mike called.

Yeah. No kidding, Caro thought, cramming her hat down, still trying to calm her horse.

The practice arena, also out-of-doors, was small

and crowded. Classy stopped outside the gate, lifted her head and snorted.

"It's the same practice arena as before," Caro told her horse, patting her neck. "Nothing to worry about."

But something must have been in the air, because Classy took two steps in and immediately bolted.

"What the—"

"They're full of themselves tonight," Mike said, loping by. His body looked too big for his tiny horse.

"I see that."

Just warm her up. She'll settle down.

But Classy didn't settle down. Maybe it was the tension in the air. This was the first night of the NFR and you could practically feel the energy crackling in the air. Maybe it was the wind. All Caro knew was that she had her hands full the entire warm-up, so much so that she didn't speak a word to any of her fellow competitors.

By the time they called for the barrel racers she was trying hard not to panic. Classy was wet with sweat. She arched her back, her head held high. Every three or four steps she let out a snort.

Equine meltdown.

Caro had experienced the phenomenon before. Nothing she did could stop the train wreck that was her coming performance. If it'd been anything other than the NFR, she'd have tipped her hat and gone back to the barn.

"Easy there, girl. Easy."

"'Luck," someone called when Caro stopped Classy in the staging area. She had no idea who'd said it because her mare had splayed her legs in front of an oncoming horse, acting like she'd never seen one of her own kind before.

Caro started to laugh. It was hysteria, she knew but she couldn't seem to stop herself. The gate man with the walkie-talkie looked at her as if she was nuts, especially when Classy tried to bolt again. Caro nearly doubled over with laughter when she'd gotten her horse under control.

"This is going to be interesting," she said to the man, who gave her a puzzled smile in return.

"You're up," he said a moment later.

She kicked Classy forward. The mare wouldn't go. Caro giggled. "Come on, girl." But there was still no putting her in drive.

"Need some help?" the gate man asked.

"No, actually—"

He slapped Classy in the rear.

"Son of a—"

It was like she'd been shot from a sling. Suddenly she was full speed ahead, but without any control. Classy ran down the long chute as if a slaughter truck were at her rear. Caro bit back another laugh, because this was unreal…just unreal. It felt like a bad dream, especially when Classy took three steps into the arena and then…stopped.

Caro almost came off. The damn saddle horn

rammed her in the gut. She gasped, using Classy's mane to hang on. Thousands of rodeo fans went quiet. Later, she'd think back and remember the arena's yellow walls brightly lit, the flash of camera bulbs, and then the quiet.

She straightened in her saddle and waved, then smiled. And laughed, even though it hurt to do so after getting nailed in the stomach. She heard people laugh with her, and then she was spurring Classy forward, her horse acting as if she'd never seen barrels before.

It became a battle of wills. Caro was determined to get them around each and every obstacle. The rodeo fans were right there with her. They applauded when, finally, she made it around the first barrel, Classy trotting the whole way. The second barrel was better; the audience voiced their approval. The third barrel wasn't bad, if she'd been competing in the Future Barrel Racers class—ages six-and-under division. Caro was pretty certain they'd walked a few steps. The audience loved it, though. They felt bad for her and were cheering for her to make it around. When she finally loped through the timing light, the place vibrated with applause. Caro lifted her hat, acknowledging their approval.

And that was that.

First ride over. Only eight more to go.

She didn't think she could do it.

Because when the applause faded, and she was

once again outside, all Caro wanted to do was cry. World champion? She didn't have a prayer, not that she'd every really thought...

"That was interesting."

She pulled up Classy, who was now, in the perverse way of equines, utterly calm. Caro had to squint to see in the darkness, but she recognized the voice.

Her mom.

"If you ever want to show her as a stock horse, I think you'd have a shot. Don't know that I've ever seen a horse apply the brakes like that."

They were just outside the arena, fighting the cursed wind, when Caro realized she was crying.

Her mom walked up to her. Caro could read the concern in her face, see the love. "Tough luck, kiddo."

"I just want to go home," Caro said through a throat clogged with tears.

"Home," her mom said, placing a hand on Classy's neck. The mare seemed to like that. She lowered her head, her sides expanding and contracting. But she wasn't breathing hard. After their slow run around the barrels, that was to be expected.

"Home?" her mom repeated. "Caroline Winifred Sheppard, I did not raise a quitter."

Caro slipped off her horse, loosened the girth automatically, slid the reins over Classy's neck by rote. "She's too green," she said. "She's not ready."

"She was ready in New Mexico."

"That was a fluke. She didn't know any better. Now she knows what to expect, and she doesn't like it. I've seen it before."

"So you ride her through it," her mom said, stepping in front of her when Caro started to lead Classy away. "You *don't* give up."

"Why not? A couple weeks ago everyone expected me to do exactly that."

"*I* wouldn't have let you," Martha said. "And if you quit now you'll break my heart."

Caro looked up sharply.

"You've worked so hard for this," her mom said, tipping up her chin like she used to do when Caro was a kid. It brought new tears to Caro's eyes. "But if you want to quit, maybe it's for the best."

"What do you mean?"

"Sometimes things happen for a reason. Sometimes we need something to shake us up. You've been going hell-bent for leather on this NFR quest ever since Dad died."

"He wanted me to do this," Caro said softly.

There were only parking lights around them, but Caro could see the compassion in her mom's eyes. "Yeah, but do *you* want to do this?"

"Of course. I always promised him I'd—"

"Do *you* want to do this?"

Caro opened her mouth to answer. Only she couldn't. She felt the blood drain from her face because she *couldn't say yes.*

"Your father wanted you to be happy, Caro. He didn't want you chasing a dream that wasn't yours. He was thrilled to have you in school, making good grades, working toward a career you really wanted. Don't do this for him. Not if you don't want to."

"But I *do* want to."

But did she?

Did she *really?*

"And I'll tell you something else," Martha said, the wind setting free some of her upswept hair. "That Ty Harrison is a nice young man. You shouldn't be so quick to let him go."

"Mom—"

"Nope. I've said my piece. The rest is up to you. Ride tomorrow or not, we'll all love you either way. But don't quit because your horse is acting bad. That's just plain silly."

Caro nodded, feeling as if she were five years old.

"I'll see you later," Martha said, giving her a hug.

"I think I'll hang out here," Caro answered. She looked her square in the eye. "I want to practice Classy around some barrels."

Martha smiled. "That's my girl."

Chapter Twenty

"Is she okay?"

Caro froze, her hand on the latch of Classy's stall. The overhead lights illuminated Ty's concern and sympathy.

"She's fine." Caro took a deep breath. "They let me work her inside. She settled down after a while."

Ty nodded. Even though it was late, he still wore his sport coat and cowboy hat, making Caro wonder if he'd even gone back to his hotel after the performance had ended. That was well over two hours ago.

"Listen, Caro, if you need a new horse, Harrison's Boots will buy you one."

Caro leaned against the stall door. She had to swallow to clear the lump in her throat. "I was going to find you tonight, after I was done here."

He tipped his head sideways, raised an eyebrow. "You were?"

She clenched her hands, taking another deep breath. "I want to apologize."

"For what?"

"For dismissing you from my life."

"You don't need to apologize. I understand how important winning the NFR is to you."

More important than me. The words were unspoken, but Caro heard them nonetheless.

"And, see, that's just it," she said, pressing her hand against the door. "Even though I told you to get lost, you're still putting me first. While I put everyone—my family, my friends, *you*—last."

"Don't judge yourself harshly," Ty said. "A lot of athletes need that focus."

"Yeah, well, my horse is the marathon runner. Or at least he used to be."

Ty took a step toward her. "That was tough luck."

"And I blamed it on you."

"Because you were mad at yourself."

Her eyes burned. She was awed by the way he seemed to understand her. "My mom made me see that sometimes things happen for a reason. That maybe I needed something to shake me up."

"I don't know about that—"

Carp held up a hand. "No. She was right. I needed to snap out of it."

"Snap out of what?"

"This," she said, indicating the stalls around them, and the arena out behind them. "My ceaseless pursuit of the NFR."

"There's nothing wrong with being competitive."

This time she was the one to take a step, bringing her within inches of him. As she looked up, Caro felt something tumble in her heart. Why hadn't she seen it before? Why had it taken her until this very moment to recognize his devotion? He would never do anything to get in her way. There could be no man on earth better suited for her than Ty.

"I *am* competitive," she said quietly. "But it's for all the wrong reasons."

"What do you mean?"

"It goes back to my father."

"In what way?"

"We were close."

"I know," he said. "You've told me."

"No, Ty, we were *close*," she said, placing a hand on his arm. She saw the way his expression softened when she touched him, how his body seemed to relax. The same thing happened to her, but she had to be honest with him. She wanted him to know what was in her heart. He deserved that.

"My father was…my best friend. He knew everything. Who I had a crush on. My first kiss. My hopes and dreams. I was Daddy's little girl."

He nodded. "I thought as much."

"But there was always one thing he wanted for himself, one thing he tried for years to achieve. Getting to the NFR."

"Wasn't he a little old to want that?"

"This was before," she said. "Before we all came along. But he'd talk about it. He was a heeler, one of the best ones in the business, but he was never quite good enough. He had a business to run—the ranch—and he couldn't get to every rodeo. This was back in the day when they didn't limit how many rodeos you could enter a year. The guys that did it full-time, every weekend, they always made the cut. But my dad could never do that and so he missed out."

"And you decided to live his dream for him."

She nodded, her eyes glistening. "That was always the plan. I'd ride through college, take a year off, go at it full-time... And maybe, just maybe, make the NFR."

"Except he passed away before you could do that."

She nodded. "And before that, David... I *let* David get in the way, just as I used *you* as an excuse when I wasn't doing well."

"What do you mean?" he asked.

"My mom thinks I'm doing this for my dad, not for myself."

"Are you?"

"I am."

He drew himself up, and her hand fell away. "You're certain?"

"Yeah," she said, looking down. "Really dumb, huh? I'm riding my heart out for a ghost."

"There's nothing wrong with that. I shut down after my mom's death."

She raised her head in surprise.

He nodded. "It took *you* to wake me up. My father helped me realize that."

She released a breath she hadn't even known she'd been holding, her lashes flickering as she fought back tears. "We're so much alike," she said, her voice hoarse.

"We are, Caro." He cupped her face.

"Don't," she said, stepping back. "If you touch me now I'll want you to keep touching me. And if that happens I'll also want you to make love to me all night. I can't do that because I've got to get up early tomorrow. I've got to ride. As much as I've been doing this for my dad, now I need to do this for me, too."

His whole face softened. "I understand."

"And when I ride, I want you here. By my side."

"Are you sure?"

"I've never been more certain of anything in my life."

He stood perfectly still for a long moment. "Caroline," he said gently, and she could hear the pent-up emotion in his voice.

She pulled his head down and kissed him in a way Caro knew would haunt her for the rest of the night.

"I'll see you tomorrow," she said softly, caressing his cheek.

"Tomorrow," he murmured.

Tomorrow.

* * *

Tomorrow.

The word echoed in her head as she drifted off to sleep. Another day to prove to herself she could do this—for her sake.

And Ty's.

How he'd become a part of the dream, she didn't know. Except if not for Harrison's Boots, she wouldn't be here. She'd never have been able to afford a full-time season, not in the beginning when pickings were scarce. But she and Thumper had improved, and Ty and Slim had stuck with her. She'd forever be grateful for that. So, yes, she wanted to win for him, too.

He showed up two hours before her performance. She was brushing Classy when he walked up and kissed her on the back of the neck. She closed her eyes for a moment, reveling in the delicious chemistry that had always been between them, before turning her head and kissing him back.

"What can I do to help?" he finally asked.

"You could clean my tack. I like my saddle really clean. Helps me to stay on when the leather is tacky to the touch."

He nodded and then did as she asked.

A little later Martha came by. Then both her brothers and Slim. They all wanted to wish her well. Caro smiled and reassured them, growing more and more relaxed.

No matter what happened, she'd always have her family. Maybe even Ty. Even Classy, as much of a brat as she'd been, would always have a home with her. Thumper, too, once he got better, and Rand continued to reassure her that he was well on his way to recovery.

And then it was time to ride.

Ty gave her a leg up. It was dark again, the sun having set hours ago. The fluorescent lights hummed as she gathered her reins. Ty looked up at her, his blond hair mussed, his green eyes full of pride.

"Go get 'em."

She bent and kissed him on the lips, not easy to do with her cowboy hat on. "I will."

Caro clucked Classy forward. The mare seemed in a better frame of mind tonight. Of course, it wasn't as windy as it had been the day before. There were no blowups on the way over to the practice pen. It was like New Mexico, only better. It didn't matter that she would go next to last, when the arena was churned up by the other horses, the footing unstable. Tonight, everything was all right.

Ty walked with her to the arena, pulling out a treat when they made it to the staging area.

"Don't give her that," Caro said, seeing the sugar cube in the palm of his hand.

He glanced up and smiled. "Why not? Might make her go faster."

"She'll be sucking on it in the arena."

"Perfect. I'm hoping it'll keep her mind off last night."

"Shh, don't remind her," Caro said, leaning forward as if to plug her mare's ears.

"Nah, she's already forgotten about last night," he said, holding out his palm. Classy sniffed the sugar cube, then lapped it up. She chewed on it so hard Caro could hear the bit clinking against her teeth.

"Now you've done it," she said, marveling at how calm she felt.

"You're up," the gate man said.

Caro straightened. "Good luck," Ty said.

She bent and kissed him again. "Don't need luck," she said, giving him a cocky smile. "Not tonight."

He stepped back as she spurred Classy forward. The mare broke into a lope. She sauntered along, ears cocked forward.

"And here comes the little lady who had a heap of trouble with her horse yesterday," said the announcer, clearly audible even though they'd yet to make the last turn to the arena.

"Yeah, Bill," said a second announcer. "A few of us here were wondering if she'd even make it all the way around…."

"Go," Caro whispered, leaning forward.

Classy went.

They burst into the arena, to the surprise of both announcers. "Wow, look at that horse go. Caroline Sheppard must have put something in that mare's oats."

That was all she heard before focusing on the first barrel. Classy saw it, too, her ears pricked forward, head up—until they started their turn. Then the mare tilted left, her body close to the ground, and expertly circled the barrel.

"That's it," Caro told her mount. "See? Nothing to worry about."

The mare lengthened her stride as Caro aimed for the second barrel. Three. Two.

Her knee hit. Caro gasped, reached out, tried to stop the thing from tipping. But they were already past. Damn it. Had it fallen? She couldn't look behind her to find out, had to focus on the next and final barrel.

"There it is, girl," she murmured, reins taut as she tried to slow Classy. "Easy."

Three. Two…

Around they went, a smile breaking out on Caro's face when she saw that the second barrel was still standing.

"Go, baby, go," she urged as they ran down the long stretch. Her butt hit the saddle, they ran so hard, and her hat nearly fell off her head. Caro had to reach up and hold it as they burst through the timing lights.

"And that's fast time," she heard the announcer say.

"With only one more rider to go," the second one added.

Fast time.

Would it hold up? She slowed Classy to a trot.

Only one rider remained in the staging area: Melanie. Caro called good luck as she brought her horse to a halt, but doubted her friend heard. She was too focused on her run.

Melanie. It *would* have to be Melanie. She was one of the best. The favorite to win the average.

Caro let Classy walk, loosening her reins as she listened to the crowd. She waited to hear groans from the arena, a sure indication that a barrel had fallen. Or an extra loud cheer, suggesting the opposite was true, that Melanie had beaten her time.

The crowd went wild.

"What is it?" Ty asked, arriving at her side out of breath. "I left right after your run. Did she beat your time?"

"I don't know," Caro said, turning to the exit tunnel. Was she done already? Damn it. The suspense was killing her. She dismounted, her hands shaking as she loosened the girth.

The crowd erupted again.

Melanie was having a good run. Over the sound of the cheers Caro could hear the hum of the announcers' voices, but it was impossible to make them out over the roar of the crowd.

Another burst of noise erupted.

"Caro, it's okay," Ty said, stepping closer.

She looked up and he smiled. "Win or lose, I'll still love you."

"You love me?" she asked, her heart pounding, although from her ride or because of his words, she didn't know.

"I think I fell in love with you the moment I saw you riding Thumper. You were so beautiful up on that horse and so kind to him when he was acting up. I could see it in your touch, hear it in your voice—your good heart."

"Oh, Ty."

Her lips trembled, her eyes welling with tears. "I love you," he said softly, bending to kiss her.

She pulled back before their lips could connect. "I love you, too."

She slipped off her horse and then he was kissing her, his lips pressed against her own with such passion and abandon Caro forgot where they were.

Until she heard a horse gallop by.

"Congratulations!" Melanie pulled her horse up. "You won." And her rival's smile couldn't have been bigger if she'd won the round herself.

"No!" Caro squeaked.

"Yep," Mel said. "But I'll get you tomorrow."

Caro squealed. The gate man offered his congratulations.

"You need to mount back up and go on out," he said.

The victory ride. Oh, yeah.

Ty hugged her once, then let her go. Smiling, Caro swung into the saddle and clucked to Classy, guiding her forward.

She would never forget what happened next. The flag bearers rode out of the tunnel ahead of her, the crowd cheering, the pennants crackling. Classy took it all in stride, looking around as if curious what all the fuss was about.

Perfect.

That's what it was. A perfect moment, made even more perfect when Caro rode back out of the tunnel afterward and saw her family standing there outside the arena. Her mom, with tears in her eyes. Rand and Jessie. Nick and Ali. Slim. All the people who mattered.

"You did it," someone yelled.

She *had* done it.

"Congratulations," Ty said when she slipped off her horse and into his arms.

"Now you'll have to win tomorrow night, too," Rand said.

"And the next night after that," Nick added.

"No," she said, tipping her head back and looking into Ty's eyes. "I've already won something more important."

And as he bent and kissed her, she knew it was true. She'd won something far more important.

Ty's heart.

Epilogue

It was the wedding of the year, held in early winter, when the air was crisp and the lake behind the altar reflected the neon-blue cloudless sky. All of Los Molinos had been invited, and the guests were now sitting in folding chairs placed on a slight incline near the shoreline.

"Would everyone please stand?" the officiate said when he caught sight of the surrey carriage pulling the bride toward her groom. In the harness, a paint horse shook his head, as if not certain he liked his new job. But with a snort of long-suffering perseverance, he trotted down the pebbled path, his black tail high, his neck arched and nostrils flaring.

It was an important day, Flora Montgomery thought. She couldn't believe that after all the planning (one hundred guests!), fretting (would it rain?) and waiting (it had to have been the world's *longest* engagement) the day had finally arrived.

"She looks good," Flora said, leaning toward her best friend, Edith.

Edith Reynolds was one of the Los Molinos "Biddie Brigade." Flora was a card-carrying member, too. She'd had the local printer emboss business cards.

"I know," Edith said, dabbing at her eyes, her long gray hair coiled on top of her head. "And I'm just so happy for her." She blew into a white handkerchief with an audible toot.

"Lovely," Flora muttered, arching a red eyebrow.

"Bite me," Edith answered, much to Flora's shock.

The bride, with a wide smile on her face, stepped down from the carriage, her long-sleeved ivory gown trailing behind her.

"She looks *happy,*" Amanda Beringer noted from her position a few pews back from the altar.

Scott, her husband, nodded, his eyes suspiciously bright. "Yes, she does."

Next to them, their son tipped forward, ignoring his little sister and the people who stood next to his parents so he could stick his tongue out at Rose Cavenaugh a couple rows back.

Chase, Rose's father, nudged his daughter. Rose rolled her eyes and then shook her head as if to say, *Boys. Blah.*

Above her head, Chase caught his wife's eye.

"Remember when we were married?" Lani asked, clearly having missed the whole exchange.

"Best day of my life," he whispered, smiling down

at her. Their six-year-old son glanced up at him and grinned. His mother's grin, Chase thought fondly.

And at the altar, standing next to the silver-haired groom, Ty leaned toward his father. "I still think we should have brought in the fake snow."

Slim's lips twitched, but his eyes never left his bride.

Martha Sheppard.

After a three-year courtship, they were finally tying the knot, and Ty couldn't have been happier. Caro looked as radiant as the bride in her gown, the ice blue perfectly complementing her eyes. She'd grown more beautiful as the years passed—if such a thing were possible. And not a day went by that he didn't thank the Lord above that he'd met her and then married her.

She turned her head and caught him staring.

I love you, his expression conveyed.

I love you, too.

They'd married the year before, exactly six months after Caroline had won the average at the NFR. Ty had proved he could run Harrison's Boots at the same time she could have a rodeo career. It'd taken some juggling, but they'd done it. Caro used the family ranch in Wyoming as a home base. Of course, she'd be home more often nowadays. She hadn't officially retired— oh, no, that wouldn't happen for a long time yet—but she was taking some time off.

For their baby.

Caro patted her stomach, the bulge plainly noticeable beneath the satin gown.

"Would everyone please be seated," the pastor intoned.

Martha stopped before her groom, her hands shaking as she handed Caro her bouquet.

"You look beautiful," Caro whispered.

"Not bad for an old lady," Martha said before pulling back and meeting the eyes of her groom.

Caro's eyes filled with tears.

After all these years her mother would be a wife again. How miraculous that two women would fall in love with men from the same family. And that her mother would find a second love—the sweetest kind.

"Dearly beloved," Pastor Rick began, "we're gathered her today…"

The words faded away as, once again, Caro caught her husband's eye. She wanted to wrap her arms around him, but she couldn't do that. Not now. So she smiled at him instead. When he smiled back, tears sparkled in his eyes, which made *her* start to cry. That, of course, started everyone in the front row to well up, including Rand, who sat next to his wife, Jessie, and their two children. Caro saw Nick tear up, too, his wife Ali gazing down at their infant son.

There wasn't a dry eye around by the time the ceremony ended and the groom kissed his bride.

"Throw the bouquet," someone called after Martha and Slim had climbed back into the carriage.

Martha clutched the skirts of her off-white gown and then complied, tossing the roses and lilies up high where it seemed to hang in the air before falling on Flora's head. She tried to bat the thing away, much to everyone's amusement, saying, "I don't want the darn thing." But no one would take it from her.

"You're next," Martha called before the driver flicked the reins.

"I *am not,*" Flora said, exasperated, still trying to off-load the thing.

"Yes, you are," Edith cried, laughing and applauding and dancing a little jig.

The crowd who followed the wedding party back up to the main house was a merry one. Leaves littered the ground, the air was chill, but nobody noticed—certainly not the bride and groom.

"Happy?" Ty asked, hanging back.

Caro nodded, misty-eyed. Geez. Would she ever stop crying? Must be hormones. "More than I've ever been in my life."

"Naw. That can't be," he teased.

"It's true."

His eyebrows hiked up. "Happier than when you won the average at the NFR?"

"Which time?" Caro asked, teasing him right back.

"The first time, of course."

"Hmm. I'm not so sure anything could top that."

"No?"

"Well…" she said, "…maybe *one* thing."

"And what's that?" Ty paused on the path. The lake sparkled behind them.

"Kiss me," she said, her laughter fading.

"Gladly."

And, yes, Caro thought, Ty's kisses were better than any NFR title. Better, even, than winning the coveted belt buckled twice, once on Classy and once on Thumper. More exciting even than Thumper being named Horse of the Year. *Nothing* was better than being in Ty's arms.

"I love you," he whispered, sending tingles down her arms.

"I love you, too," Caro said, snuggling into him.

And as she looked out at the land that surrounded the Diamond W, she was filled with happiness. It was a happiness shared by her brothers and their wives, and their children. And many, many years later, it would be shared by their children's children. A happiness that would linger over the Diamond W and Los Molinos for generations to come.

* * * * *

THE ROYAL HOUSE OF NIROLI
Always passionate, always proud

The richest royal family in the world—united by
blood and passion, torn apart by deceit and desire

Nestled in the azure blue of the Mediterranean Sea, the
majestic island of Niroli has prospered for centuries.
The Fierezza men have worn the crown with passion
and pride since ancient times. But now, as the king's
health declines, and his two sons have been tragically
killed, the crown is in jeopardy.

The clock is ticking—a new heir must be found
before the king is forced to abdicate. By royal decree
the internationally scattered members of the Fierezza
family are summoned to claim their destiny. But any
person who takes the throne must do so according to
The Rules of the Royal House of Niroli. Soon secrets
and rivalries emerge as the descendents of this ancient
royal line vie for position and power. Only a true
Fierezza can become ruler—a person dedicated to
their country, their people…and their eternal love!

Each month starting in July 2007,
Harlequin Presents is delighted to bring you
an exciting installment from
THE ROYAL HOUSE OF NIROLI,
in which you can follow the epic search
for the true Nirolian king.
Eight heirs, eight romances, eight fantastic stories!

Here's your chance to enjoy a sneak preview of the
first book delivered to you by royal decree…

FIVE minutes later she was standing immobile in front of the study's window, her original purpose of coming in forgotten, as she stared in shocked horror at the envelope she was holding. Waves of heat followed by icy chill surged through her body. She could hardly see the address now through her blurred vision, but the crest on its left-hand front corner stood out, its *royal* crest, followed by the address: *HRH Prince Marco of Niroli…*

She didn't hear Marco's key in the apartment door, she didn't even hear him calling out her name. Her shock was so great that nothing could penetrate it. It encased her in a kind of bubble, which only concentrated the torment of what she was suffering and branded it on her brain so that it could never be forgotten. It was only finally pierced by the sudden opening of the study door as Marco walked in.

"Welcome home, *Your Highness*. I suppose I

ought to curtsy." She waited, praying that he would laugh and tell her that she had got it all wrong, that the envelope she was holding, addressing him as Prince Marco of Niroli, was some silly mistake. But like a tiny candle flame shivering vulnerably in the dark, her hope trembled fearfully. And then the look in Marco's eyes extinguished it as cruelly as a hand placed callously over a dying person's face to stem their last breath.

"Give that to me," he demanded, taking the envelope from her.

"It's too late, Marco," Emily told him brokenly. "I know the truth now…." She dug her teeth into her lower lip to try to force back her own pain.

"You had no right to go through my desk," Marco shot back at her furiously, full of loathing at being caught off-guard and forced into a position in which he was in the wrong, making him determined to find something he could accuse Emily of. "I trusted you…."

Emily could hardly believe what she was hearing. "No, you didn't trust me, Marco, and you didn't trust me because you knew that I couldn't trust you. And you knew that because you're a liar, and liars don't trust people because they know that they themselves cannot be trusted." She not only felt sick, she also felt as though she could hardly breathe. "You are Prince Marco of Niroli…. How could you not tell me who you are and still live with me as intimately as we have lived together?" she demanded brokenly.

"Stop being so ridiculously dramatic," Marco demanded fiercely. "You are making too much of the situation."

"*Too much?*" Emily almost screamed the words at him. "When were you going to tell me, Marco? Perhaps you just planned to walk away without telling me anything? After all, what do my feelings matter to you?"

"Of course they matter." Marco stopped her sharply. "And it was in part to protect them, and you, that I decided not to inform you when my grandfather first announced that he intended to step down from the throne and hand it on to me."

"To protect me?" Emily nearly choked on her fury. "Hand on the throne? No wonder you told me when you first took me to bed that all you wanted was sex. You *knew* that was the only kind of relationship there could ever be between us! You *knew* that one day you would be Niroli's king. No doubt you are expected to marry a princess. Is she picked out for you already, your *royal* bride?"

* * * * *

Look for
THE FUTURE KING'S PREGNANT MISTRESS
by Penny Jordan in July 2007,
from Harlequin Presents,
available wherever books are sold.

Mediterranean
N I G H T S™

Experience the glamour and elegance of cruising the
high seas with a new 12-book series....

MEDITERRANEAN NIGHTS

Coming in July 2007...

SCENT OF A
WOMAN

by

Joanne Rock

When Danielle Chevalier is invited to an exclusive
conference aboard *Alexandra's Dream*, she knows it
will mean good things for her struggling fragrance
company. But her dreams get a setback when she
meets Adam Burns, a representative from a large
American conglomerate.

Danielle is charmed by the brusque American—
until she finds out he means to compete with her bid
for the opportunity that will save her family business!

HM38961

Do you know a real-life heroine?

Nominate her for the Harlequin More Than Words award.

Each year Harlequin Enterprises honors five ordinary women for their extraordinary commitment to their community.

Each recipient of the Harlequin More Than Words award receives a $10,000 donation from Harlequin to advance the work of her chosen charity. And five of Harlequin's most acclaimed authors donate their time and creative talents to writing a novella inspired by the award recipients. The More Than Words anthology is published annually in October and all proceeds benefit causes of concern to women.

HARLEQUIN

More Than Words

For more details or to nominate a woman you know please visit

www.HarlequinMoreThanWords.com

nocturne™

**DON'T MISS THE RIVETING CONCLUSION
TO THE RAINTREE TRILOGY**

RAINTREE: SANCTUARY

by *New York Times* bestselling author

BEVERLY
BARTON

Mercy, guardian of the Raintree
homeplace, takes a stand against
the Ansara wizards to battle for
the Clan's future.

*On sale July,
wherever books are sold.*

SNRT2

THE GARRISONS
A brand-new family saga begins with

THE CEO'S SCANDALOUS AFFAIR
BY ROXANNE ST. CLAIRE

Eldest son Parker Garrison is preoccupied running
his Miami hotel empire and dealing with his recently
deceased father's secret second family. Since he has
little time to date, taking his superefficient assistant
to a charity event should have been a simple plan.
Until passion takes them beyond business.

**Don't miss any of the six exciting titles in
THE GARRISONS continuity, beginning in July.
Only from Silhouette Desire.**

THE CEO'S SCANDALOUS AFFAIR
#1807

Available July 2007.

REQUEST YOUR FREE BOOKS!
2 FREE NOVELS PLUS 2
FREE GIFTS!

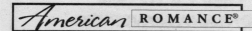

American **ROMANCE®**

Heart, Home & Happiness!

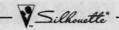

SPECIAL EDITION™

Look for six new
MONTANA MAVERICKS
stories, beginning in July with

THE MAN WHO HAD EVERYTHING

by CHRISTINE RIMMER

When Grant Clifton decided to sell the
family ranch, he knew it would devastate
Stephanie Julen, the caretaker who'd always been
like a little sister to him. He wanted a new start,
but how could he tell her that she and her mother
would have to leave...especially now that he was
head over heels in love with her?

MONTANA MAVERICKS

Dreaming big—and winning hearts—in Big Sky Country

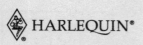

COMING NEXT MONTH

#1169 THE RANCHER NEXT DOOR by Cathy Gillen Thacker
Texas Legacies: The Carrigans

Rebecca Carrigan expects her alpaca farm will rile the local cattlemen, especially after she practically steals her property right out from under the nose of Trevor McCabe. Trevor's interest is definitely piqued by his beautiful neighbor—and when she is seen on the arm of his archrival, the whole town knows that's like waving a red flag in front of a bull!

#1170 TROUBLE IN TENNESSEE by Tanya Michaels
In the Family

Treble "Trouble" James isn't thrilled about returning to her hometown of Joyous, Tennessee, but her sister, pregnant with her first child, needs her. Thankfully, confronting the people who had judged her youthful, wild behavior is easier after meeting Dr. Keith Caldwell, a man who has a soft spot for trouble. Together they create quite a bit of their own!

#1171 HOME TO THE DOCTOR by Mary Anne Wilson
Shelter Island Stories

Holed up to nurse a broken leg, tough-minded businessman Ethan Grace never expected challenges of any sort at his estate on Shelter Island, in the Pacific Ocean, off Puget Sound. Then again, he hadn't yet run into now-grown-up lady doctor Morgan Kelly, smart, beautiful, intriguing—and determined not to let the powerful Grace conglomerate do her father in...no matter how drawn to Ethan she is.

#1172 TEMPORARILY TEXAN by Victoria Chancellor
Brody's Crossing

When a mix-up lands gardening consultant Raven York deep in the heart of Texas cattle country, the strictly vegetarian Yankee is horrified to find herself bunking down with a meat-eating all-American cowboy. She thinks that tofu is healthier than a T-bone, but what about the animal attraction she feels for him?

HARCNM0607